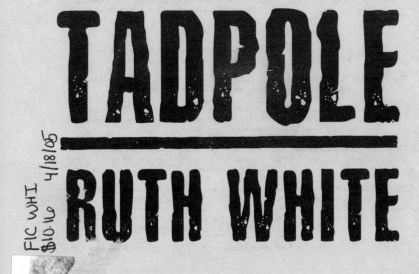

TADPOLE

RUTH WHITE

NORTHEASTERN
MIDDLE SCHOOL LIBRARY

A DELL YEARLING BOOK

Published by
Dell Yearling
an imprint of
Random House Children's Books
a division of Random House, Inc.
New York

Visit us on the Web! www.randomhouse.com/kids

Educators and librarians, for a variety of teaching tools, visit us at www.randomhouse.com/teachers

ISBN: 0-440-41979-4

Reprinted by arrangement with Farrar, Straus and Giroux

Printed in the United States of America

December 2004

10 9 8 7 6 5 4 3 2 1

OPM

FOR "TOAD"

TADPOLE

1

ONE DAY IN JUNE, Mama found this ad in the paper: *permanent waves one $ Sat morn come early.* And there was an address for a boardinghouse on Bee Street in Riverbend.

"It's the only way we'll ever get curly hair," Mama proclaimed, "and don't my girls deserve to look as good as the town girls do?"

We agreed that it was so. Mama's girls deserved such a treat. So on Saturday morning we got up early and walked to the highway to catch the eight o'clock bus into town.

Striding tall in front of Mama, Kentucky led the way. She was fourteen that summer of 1955, the oldest and most popular of the four of us. Everybody loved Kentucky Collins. Sometimes she was called Ken.

Virginia followed beside Mama. At twelve, she was the prettiest. She turned heads wherever she went. Sometimes we called her Gin.

Behind Virginia and Mama, Georgia walked with me. Georgia was eleven, and the smartest. She made straight O's—for outstanding—on her report card every grading period.

We were a mixed-up batch of English, Scotch-Irish, and German, with a little dab of Cherokee Indian throwed in on our daddy's side, which did not take, for we all had blond hair and blue eyes, fair skin and little bitty feet.

By eight-thirty we were knocking on the door of the boardinghouse. A redheaded fat woman with bags under her eyes peeped out at us. She had not had her morning coffee, so she said we'd have to wait.

"Y'all just set down out here," she told us, tossing her red head toward the porch. "And I'll be wid'ja in a jiffy."

So we did what she told us to. We set down. The porch was long and shady, with lots of rocking chairs and gliders for the guests.

"How come we gotta wait?" Virginia complained, and whenever Virginia Collins complained, she did it loud.

In fact, LOUD was a word describing all of my sisters, and me too. We talked loud. We laughed loud. We cried loud. We quarreled loud. We sung loud. Yes, I'll have to admit that we were known near and far as "them loud-mouthed Collins gals."

"Didn't the paper say come early?" Virginia wailed.

"That's right," Georgia said. "The paper did say come early. Well, here we are!"

"You put me in mind of Tadpole when you said that!"

That come from me, Carolina, the ten-year-old runt, sometimes called Carol, and nobody at all.

As usual, the mention of our favorite cousin, Tadpole Birch, shut everybody up, if only for a moment, and sent us into private pleasant memories.

After a time Virginia broke the silence. "Yeah, he's always saying, 'Well, here we are!' " She opened her arms wide and chuckled.

"Mama, when can we see Tadpole again?" I said. (Maybe I whined.)

"I don't know, Carol. Since he moved in with his aunt and uncle at Feds Creek—well, you know, that's twenty-five miles down the river—and the Birches don't go much."

Mama was just Mama. She was not loud. She worked in the kitchen of the Riverbend Hospital, cooking, washing dishes, and serving food to the sick people. She was the only mother we knew who got up every morning, except Saturday, and went to work.

"They don't go at all," Kentucky said. "Poor Tadpole."

"Yeah, poor Tadpole," Virginia agreed. "He loves to go places and see people, and there he is stuck with that old sourpuss and her tightwad husband. They don't ever crack a smile."

"They go to bed at sunset so they won't have to burn the lights," Georgia said.

"And they get up at the crack of dawn," I added, "to milk the cows, and feed the chickens and the pigs, and work in the fields."

"Poor Tadpole," we agreed.

When Tadpole was three years old, his mama, who was our mama's favorite sister, had died with the TB. A year later his daddy, who was a Birch, was killed in a mining accident.

Nobody had wanted to keep that poor li'l ole orphan boy, and ever since he had been tossed around from one relative to another—a month here, three months there, six months someplace else.

Except for short visits from Tadpole now and then, Mama never was on the circuit. With four girls to tend to by herself, she had her hands full, and nobody in the family had the heart to ask her to help.

But she had some opinions just the same. For instance, she thought it was mighty fishy that as soon as Tadpole had turned thirteen in the spring, his Uncle Matthew Birch had suddenly wanted him permanent.

"It's because he's old enough to work," she declared with some bitterness. "They'll work that poor boy to death."

But the rest of the relatives were glad to be shed of the responsibility, and asked no questions.

"We'll sign him over to Matthew, make it legal," they all agreed.

Matthew Birch was Tadpole's daddy's brother. His wife's name was Lucy, and they used to have a boy the same age as Tadpole, but he died mysteriously when he was real young.

We hadn't seen Tadpole since last April, when Uncle Daniel brung him to spend Easter Sunday with us. Shortly after that he went to live with the Birches.

"Remember how he got his nickname?" I said. "He was down at the creek, and somebody dared him—"

"Let me tell it!" Virginia butted in. "You'll mess it up."

I yielded the floor like always, and Virginia picked up the story.

"He was down at the creek with two of Uncle Luther's boys."

"Yeah, it was Bruce and Walter," Georgia said.

"They were damming up the water or something like that," Virginia went on, "and Tadpole mentioned that he was so hungry he could eat a mess of tadpoles."

"No, Bruce said that first!" Kentucky interrupted. "That's how it started. And so Tadpole told him, 'I dare you to ketch one and eat it.' "

"No, Walter dared Tadpole!" Georgia joined the argument.

"Anyhow, somebody dared somebody." I squeezed in a word sideways.

"Bruce and Walter dared Tadpole to swallow one of them tadpoles live," Georgia cried. "And he did!"

"An hour later he threw it up, and . . ." Kentucky yelled above everybody else.

". . . it was still alive!" we all squealed together.

There was muffled laughter from inside the house.

"Sh . . . hh," Mama said, putting her finger to her lips, but she couldn't keep the corners of her own mouth from curling up.

"Still alive," Virginia repeated with a smile.

"Yessiree," Kentucky added. "He said it was still flipping its tail. So they throwed it back in the creek."

"And he's been Tadpole ever since," Georgia said.

"What was his real name, Mama?" I said. "I forgit."

"Winston Churchill Birch," said Mama, with pride.

The four of us looked at each other, rolled our eyes, and bellowed, "Tadpole!"

The screen door flew open and the red head popped out.

"Okay, who's first?"

We spent the next coupla hours being tortured with curling rods and permanent solutions that blistered our scalps, and hair dryers so hot we had to fan each other with cardboard fans. But it was for beauty's sake.

The red head turned out to be a real beautician with a license and all, from Pikeville, and right clever about how to make a buck from these hillbillies in Riverbend.

When we were done, we went outside and gulped fresh air, all of us as frizzy-headed as poodles, stinking of permanent solution, and with necks and ears that would glow in the dark. Red Head was working at fever pitch on five people behind us, and three more were waiting on the porch.

Without a word, them three watched us five strutting proudly by in our new dos.

"Early bird gets the worm," Virginia said prissily as she patted her curly head.

One of the women giggled behind her summer gloves. Another one promptly stood up and beat us down the steps. In a minute she had disappeared up Bee Street.

That shut us up—but only for a minute. We looked at each other, and shrugged. It was plain the woman had no taste.

"That didn't take as long as I thought," Mama said when we were on the street. "It's only eleven-thirty."

"Let's go to the show," I begged.

"Oh, let's do." Georgia joined my team. "*Rebel Without a Cause* is playing! It's got James Dean in it!"

Kentucky and Virginia didn't say anything. They were waiting to see how Mama would respond. We were headed toward River Street, where the movie theater was.

"We can't," Mama said at last.

"Why not?" we all cried.

"Name me one good reason!" Georgia said crossly.

"I can name lots of reasons," Mama said with a sigh. "Starting with those permanents. That was five dollars. Then there's the light bill that's already past due, and there's the insurance premium, and we owe Pugh's Mercantile where we've been charging groceries—"

"You always do that!" I said crankily.

"Yeah, the minute we ast for something, you start reciting a list of *bills!*" Georgia said, spitting out the word *bills*, like it put a bad taste in her mouth.

"The bills always get paid somehow, don't they?" Virginia said.

"Yeah, they do!" Kentucky said.

"So they'll get paid this time, too!" I added.

Mama hushed. We had won. Poor Mama! She hadn't a chance against the four of us. When I was two, our daddy had left her all alone to do for us the best she could. Sure, he had been proud enough to help her bring us into the world. He was the one who gave us these highfalutin names for states he'd been to. But then he left for one of those states, or somewheres else, and no one had seen him since. I was the only one who had no memory of him.

"Why'd he go?" I asked over and over again to anybody who usta know him.

Some people made like comedians and said, "To get away from y'all."

Others shrugged and said, "I don't know."

Or they said, "Nobody knows."

Mama said, "He was tired."

Tired? What does that mean? You get tired and you take a nap. Then you're over it. You don't leave forever 'cause you're tired, for crying out loud!

We took our time strolling past the dime store and the drugstore, looking at ourselves in the glass. We held our heads a little higher, and patted our curls.

Rebel Without a Cause was to start at noon. We bought tickets and went into a lighted theater and seated ourselves right in the middle. There were plenty of folks around us when we sat down, but when the reel got to rolling good, I noticed they moved away from us and settled along the walls.

When we started whining for popcorn and fountain Cokes, Mama gave us the money without a word. We heard nothing about all the bills she had to pay. It was a miracle.

After the movie, which was real good, we took the Black and White Transit back up the river that curled through the Kentucky hills, toward home. We got off at the mouth of Polly's Fork and walked a mile up the holler, where we lived in a tiny but tidy brown house. We had a kitchen, a living room, and two bedrooms with two beds in each one, our own well outside, a small back porch, and a larger front porch, where we spent a lot of time in warm weather.

We were just about give out, and rounding the last curve before home, when we heard it—guitar music, and singing.

Got a feeling called the blu . . . uu . . . ues, oh, Lord,
Since my baby said goodbye.
I don't know what I'm gonna do . . . oo,
All I do is sit and sigh.

My sisters and me, we ran, forgetting how tired we were. And there he was sitting on our front porch, picking and singing. Our neighbors, the Pughs and the McCoys, were gathered in our yard.

I've grown so used to you, somehow,
But I'm nobody's sugar daddy now,
And I'm lo . . . oo . . . onesome,
I've got the love-sick blues!

Oh, yeah, it was our favorite person in the world come for a visit. Tadpole grinned real big when he saw us, and opened his arms wide.

"Well, here we are!"

2

"*HOWDY! HOWDY! HOWDY!*" The greetings flowed as we welcomed him noisily.

"Speak of the Devil and he appears!" Kentucky's voice rose above everybody else's, as she slapped Tadpole on the back.

"Who're you calling a devil?" Tadpole responded with a playful punch to her arm.

"Yeah, it's funny we were just talking about you a while ago," Virginia said.

"I know! My ears were burning something awful," he came back.

"Ain't that the way it always goes?" Mrs. Pugh said. "Maybe you don't see a person for ages, or even think of 'em, and then one day they pop into your head, and next thing you know they appear."

"I've noticed that myself," Mrs. McCoy agreed.

Picking themselves up to leave, the neighbors said things like, "You sound 'zactly like Hank Williams, boy."

And, "You kinda favor him, too."

Yeah, he did a little bit.

Then they walked up the holler toward their houses, and let us be alone with our kin.

It seemed like Tadpole had growed six inches since we last saw him at Easter. Spindly and suntanned, he was as good-looking as ever. His hair was black and curly, his twinkling eyes as blue as cornflowers, and he kept a pleasant expression on his face come what may.

We settled around him on the porch and peppered him with questions.

"What're you doing here?"

"How long can you stay?"

"How'd you git here?"

To which he answered in order, "I come for a visit. I can stay for a few days. I hitched a ride with a feller who lives in Majestic."

Mama, who had been taking her time because her feet hurt, reached the house and greeted her nephew with a big hug.

He returned her hug and held on to her for a long time. Then he pulled back and hollered, "Lordy mercy! What's that stink y'all got on?"

I noticed that his eyes were shiny with unshed tears.

"Permanents!" Virginia said. "We all had permanent waves today!"

And once again she strutted like a peacock, patting her spiffy new do.

"I thought you looked kinda frizzy-headed," Tadpole said. "Will it stay like that?"

"For a while," Georgia said. "But it'll gradually relax and get straight again."

"Then how come they call it a permanent?" Tadpole said. "It orta be called a temporary."

He had brung a few changes of clothes stuffed into a pillowcase, and Mama toted it into the house with her when she went in to start supper. We stayed outside with Tadpole, acting the fool. Drek'ly Mama sent us to the garden to gather vegetables.

In warm weather we always had good things to eat, starting with the cherries in May, then the strawberries, spring lettuce, green onions, cucumbers, tomatoes. Now the green beans were coming on, and hallelujah, the roastin' ears would be ready by the Fourth of July. Also, the mulberries, blackberries, melons, peppers, potatoes, beets, and I don't know what all. Yeah, in the summertime we ate like royalty. Other times we were squirrels, relying on what we had stashed away.

We gathered lettuce, cukes, tomatoes, and green onions. Coming into the kitchen, Tadpole took off his shoes and set 'em on the back porch. I couldn't help noticing how filthy and wore out they were. He had nearabout walked the soles off.

Mama had fixed green beans, potatoes, corn bread, and side meat. She made a salad of the lettuce and onions and scalded it with drippings from the pork. She cooked on a coal stove, and we had another coal stove in the living room for winter. Coal made for cheap heating, 'cause you could chuck it right outa the hillside behind the house.

When we settled down to eat, Tadpole started gobbling up food like an old hog at the trough. It was the first time he'd stopped grinning and talking since we spotted him on the porch.

"Didn't your Aunt Lucy feed you?" Kentucky teased him.

Tadpole's mouth was so full he couldn't answer her.

"How're they doing anyhow?" Mama wanted to know.

"Ff . . . nn," Tadpole mumbled.

"And how've you been?" she went on.

He made a circle with his thumb and index finger, meaning okay.

"Did'ja pass seventh grade?" Georgia asked him.

He nodded.

"Do you like that school over there at Feds Creek?" Kentucky asked.

"Tell me about *Rebel Without a Cause*." He changed the subject as soon as he was able to talk. "James Dean is my fav'rit movie star."

While we ate, Kentucky told the whole story with a lot of help from Georgia, who couldn't let her overlook anything. Tadpole was a real good listener. He butted in only once to ask a question, and that was, "Do you got some molasses, Aunt Serilda?"

Mama fetched the molasses pitcher from the cabinet, and Tadpole drownded the rest of his supper in it.

"And then what happened?" he said, turning back to Kentucky.

When supper was done, we were chompin' at the bit to get Tadpole back outside to get on with the fun and jokes. But our cousin stayed behind in the kitchen to help Mama clean up. It's something orphans pick up when they are passed around from house to house. With low rumbles and mutterings, the rest of us helped.

"Now, let's go sing!" I said when we were finished.

And we did. For hours Tadpole sat on the front porch with his bare feet dangling over the edge, playing his guitar and singing. The bigger girls hogged him right and left, and I couldn't even get close. So I moved down on the ground in front of him. Mama came out and sat quiet in a rocking chair.

The air was sweet. The night was clear. The sky was milky with stars from one mountaintop to another. The moon was full, and hanging so low I figured you could stand up there on top of one of them mountains, and reach out and grab it.

We sang every song we knew, and some we didn't. The neighbors came and went, settling on blankets in the yard. Somebody had made up a whole mess of fudge, and somebody else brought ice cubes for us to suck on. Everybody sang along when they knew the words. Some people had requests. Tadpole could pick up a tune on that guitar faster'n anybody you ever saw. And you couldn't sing anything he couldn't play.

It was between ten and eleven before folks took to drifting away, until only the six of us were left. I had not stayed up this late many times in my life.

Tadpole yawned. "Okay, one more. Then I gotta rest my weary bones."

" 'Blue Moon of Kentucky'?" Mama's voice came soft out of the shadows.

"Good choice, Aunt Serilda." He hummed softly, searching for the right key and chords on his guitar.

Dreamily we all looked up at the moon and stars as he sang.

Blue moon of Kentucky, keep on shining.
Shine on the one that's gone and proved untrue.
Blue moon of Kentucky, keep on shining.
Shine on the one that's gone and left me blue.

It was on a moonlight night,
The stars were shining bright.
And they whispered from on high,
Your love has said goodbye.

Blue moon of Kentucky, keep on shining.
Shine on the one that's gone and said goodbye.

We were quiet as we got ready for bed. It had been a long, busy day. First we took turns going to the toilet. It was a wooden outhouse way down yonder between the garden and the creek, and Mama went with me because I was afraid to go by myself in the dark.

Then Mama fixed a bed for Tadpole on the couch. Kentucky and Virginia went to the front bedroom. In the back bedroom by the kitchen, me and Mama crawled into our bed, and Georgia into hers. Sleep came easy.

I don't know what time it was that I woke up with Tadpole standing beside our bed and whispering, "Aunt Serilda?"

He said it so soft I don't think I woulda woke up a'tall, except that he was shaking Mama's shoulder and one of his fingers got caught in my hair where I rested my head against her.

She raised up and whispered, "What is it?"

"Can you come out here for a minute?"

Then he turned and left the room. Mama got up, put on her summer robe over her nightgown, and followed him barefooted. There was a curtain hanging over the doorway separating our bedroom from the kitchen, and I saw a light come on in there. I waited and listened, but I couldn't hear a thing.

Finally, curiosity made me step light from my bed. I tiptoed to the curtain and peeped out the side where there was a crack.

Tadpole and Mama were sitting at the table, whispering. Tadpole had on his britches, but he was bare-chested. His face was toward me, and I could see that his reg'lar smile was no place to be seen. I tried to hear what they were saying, but I caught only a coupla words here and there.

". . . Uncle Matthew . . ."

". . . with a whip?"

". . . kaint go back there . . ."

". . . let me see . . ."

Tadpole turned his bare back so that Mama could see it, and so could I. I almost cried out, for there crisscrossing my cousin's back were these big old blood-red whelps.

Mama put a hand over her mouth, then

reached out for Tadpole, being careful not to hurt him. He clung to her neck and sobbed. They cried together for a few minutes, and I heard Mama say something about her poor dead sister's boy. They cried some more.

Then, drying her tears on her robe, Mama got up and went over to the cabinet, where she fumbled around in the remedies drawer and found a tin of Rosebud. She took the salve and slathered it easy over the whelps on Tadpole's back. After that, she sat back down with him, and they went on talking together.

I slipped into bed, and lay there listening. I could hear the sss . . . sss of their whisperings. I could hear Georgia breathing deep. I could hear the water rippling over the rocks in the creek.

And the blue moon of Kentucky spilled its beams over our little house in the hills.

3

THE NEXT MORNING I woke up with the thought that I knew something my sisters did not know—prob'ly for the first time ever in the world. It was an important secret between me and Mama and Tadpole.

Mama and my sisters were up a'ready, so I got outa bed and looked at my hair in the mirror over the dresser. Where I had laid on it, a deep ridge ran down the side of my head, and all the curls were pushed to either side of it. I tried to brush it shut, but it was hopeless. I ast myself then what did I want a permanent for anyhow? Why would anybody want one? But Self had no answer.

I sighed and put on my best sundress. It usta be pretty when it belonged to Kentucky. Then it wa'

Virginia's, then Georgia's. Now it was wore out. I stepped out into the world barefooted. My feet were so tough by June I coulda walked on nails. Besides, I had no ever'day summer shoes.

I think we were poor, but we didn't know it. We thought we were pretty well off. Compared to some other folks we knew, like them Jewells up on the mountain, for instance—now, you talk about poor! Well, let's just say we had plenty. But sometimes we couldn't help complaining.

"Hang me if there ain't another hole in the sleeve of this blouse," somebody walking by might hear Kentucky hollering. "My crazy bone is hanging out!"

Or, "Lordy mercy! I wisht I had me a new pair of shoes!" from Georgia. "Look at these old thangs, would'ja?"

That morning it was Virginia's turn to lament: "Wisht I had me a red sundress like the one I saw in Aldens Catalog."

"Wisht I had me some earplugs," mumbled Tadpole from his couch bed, where he was still trying to sleep with all our commotion around him.

"I wisht I had me a new dress, too!" I joined the wishing. "This one is frayed."

"What's it 'fraid of?" Tadpole wanted to know.

That's how our second day with Tadpole started—with more carrying-on.

Mama had scrambled us some eggs, baked but-termilk biscuits, and made milk gravy, all of which she left on the stove to stay warm. It was Sunday, but she was ready for work. Saturday was her only day off. Before going out the front door, she kissed us girls and gave instructions.

"Ken, wash up the breakfast dishes."

A grunt from Kentucky.

"Gin, fix tomato sandwiches for lunch."

A nod from Virginia.

"Georgia, sweep off the front porch."

An eye roll from Georgia.

"Carolina, try to stay out of the way."

A sigh from me.

"Tadpole, at about five o'clock, build me a fire in the cookstove."

"I'll do that, Aunt Serilda," Tadpole said quick, and propped his'self up on one elbow to smile at her. His wounds were against the back of the couch, so you couldn't see them.

Nobody laughed anymore at Mama's daily ad-vice for me, which was always the same—stay out of the way—but her instructions to Tadpole turned all our heads. You never asked guests to do chores! What was she thinking?

Mama left for work then. She had to walk down to the highway to catch the bus unless somebody came along and gave her a lift.

Me and my sisters went into the kitchen so Tadpole could get up and put on his clothes. We settled around the breakfast table and began to eat, without waiting for him. In a few minutes he joined us.

"Ri'cheer, Tad," I said, and patted the seat beside me. "You can set in Mama's place."

"Tad?" Tadpole said. Then a gleam came in his blue eyes, and he looked hard at me—just me—like he had suddenly discovered my existence. "I think I like that, little Carol." And he sat down beside me. "Tad—yeah, Tad Birch!"

"Why did Mama give you a chore to do, Tadpole?" Kentucky asked.

"I'll answer only to Tad from now on," he declared as he smiled at me and ruffled my bushy head. I couldn't quite swallow my breakfast, or wipe the grin off my face.

"It's a new day," he went on, "and time for a new name. I'm not crazy 'bout Winston Churchill, and Tadpole is a kid's nickname. But Tad? Yeah, it's got a nice ring to it."

"All right, then, TAD!" Kentucky yelled his name. "Mama never does ast a guest to do anything. So why'd she tell you to build 'er a fire? Are you gonna stay here?"

"For a bit," Tad spoke so quiet I barely heard him.

Then he spooned out some scrambled eggs,

crumbled biscuits on top of them, and ladled gravy over it all.

"You ain't going back to the Birches?" Virginia said.

Tad sighed. "I don't want to. I hope I don't have to."

"I don't blame you," Georgia said. "They are bor . . . ing!"

"Do they even know you're here?" Virginia narrowed her eyes at him.

"Did you run away?" asked Kentucky.

"No, they don't know I'm here, and yes, I run away," Tad answered.

At that precise moment a pickup truck could be heard lumbering up the dirt road. Tadpole's fork stopped in midair as he tilted his head to listen.

"That's the Boultons' truck," I reassured him.

He relaxed and gave me a quick smile, then poured a cup of coffee from the stove, and tipped it into his saucer to cool. All the while my sisters looked from him to each other with wide eyes. I was disappointed that he had told them so soon. But anyhow, I still had the secret about the stripes on his back.

"Whadda ya gonna do?" Georgia asked.

"I reckon I'll have to appeal to Mama's people. Aunt Serilda is gonna help me write some letters," Tadpole said. "We know I can't stay here."

"Why not?" I said.

"There's just not room for me, Carol," he said sadly. "Your mama has too many mouths to feed now."

"What if your aunt and uncle come looking for you?" Kentucky said.

"Aunt Serilda said for me to run if they try to force me to go with them."

"She did?" Georgia seemed amazed that Mama would say such a thing.

"I don't think they'll waste their gas looking for me," Tad said. "But Aunt Serilda thinks they might."

He slurped up the coffee from his saucer.

"What did they do to you?" Kentucky wanted to know.

Tad hesitated. We all eyed him, waiting for an answer.

He shrugged. "Oh, they just took my guitar away from me, that's all, said it was a waste of time."

"Oh," my sisters mumbled.

"But it's the only thing I have left of my daddy," he explained sadly. "On Friday morning, when Uncle Matthew and Aunt Lucy drove to the company store, I went looking for my guitar, and when I found it, I packed up a few things, and took off.

"I walked most all the way through the hills 'cause I was afraid Uncle Matthew would come by. There wadn't much traffic anyway, but I managed to catch a ride on the other side of Riverbend up to the mouth of the holler."

We heard the front screen door slam. From where I sat, I could see tiny Peggy McCoy coming into the living room.

"Let's keep this to ourself," Tad whispered.

Nobody ever knocked on a door in Polly's Fork. They just walked right in like they owned the place. Peggy came into the kitchen. She was only a year younger than me, but she seemed lots younger. In fact, she coulda passed for six easy.

Peggy lived up the holler a piece on the hillside with her mama and daddy, five sisters, six brothers, fourteen cows, fifty-five chickens, eleven pigs, nineteen goats, three dogs, six cats, and two mules. I knew because I had helped her count them all a few days earlier.

"Hidy, Tadpole," she said dreamily, and sidled up to him at the table.

She was wearing a pink sundress made out of a feed sack, and she had her hair in tight pigtails tied with pink ribbons. Peggy had freckles, which the two of us had tried to count that day we were counting everything else, but we didn't know any numbers that high. She was barefooted and pigeon-toed.

"My name is Tad!" he pronounced.

"Huh?" Peggy said.

"Don't call me Tadpole no more, I am Tad," he explained careful.

"Well, anyhow, Tadpole, would you wanna come up to our house to play the *git*-tar and sing on the Fourth of July?"

My sisters giggled. Peggy was the baby of the family, so we knew it was her older sisters who had put her up to this.

"How's about my cousins here?" Tad nodded his head in our direction.

"Them?" Peggy said. "They can't play the *git*-tar and sing."

"I mean are they invited, too?"

"I don't know." Peggy's expression was blank. "They didn't say nothing about them. They just said you."

"Who?" Kentucky quizzed her.

"Huh?" Peggy said.

"Who didn't say nothing about us?" Virginia wanted to know.

Peggy thought about that, then shrugged. "Nobody."

We busted out laughing.

"Okay, let's start over," Tad said. "Somebody told you to come here and invite me to your house for the Fourth of July, 'zat right?"

"Will you?" Peggy pleaded. "Please, pretty please?"

"Who sent you down here?" Virginia got to the point.

"It stinks in here," Peggy mumbled, twisting her dress tail around one hand.

"Stinks!" Kentucky was insulted. "Whadda you mean?"

"It's the permanents," Virginia reminded her. "We're used to the odor now and don't smell it, but she does."

"Anyhow"—Tad got back on track—"I'll go if my kin are invited, too."

"Huh?" Peggy said one more time.

"Go on home, Peggy," Tad said to her. "Tell them maybe."

4

TAD HELPED KENTUCKY clean up the kitchen after breakfast, then found a change of clothes and went out to draw up water from the well. He wanted an out-of-doors bath, he said. We helped him fill the tub.

"I feel downright filthy," he said. "I ain't worshed good for days. I spent Friday night sleeping under a bridge."

On what was left over from the breakfast coals, we heated the frigid water to lukewarm so Tad could stand it, and poured it into a tub. Then my sisters and me went into the house. We could hear Tad singing as he splashed around in the water.

Some time later we joined him out there again,

and lo and behold, there he was in the garden, pulling up weeds. His wet hair was just a'glistenin' in the morning sunshine.

"Feel like a new man," he said brightly.

"You're gonna get all dirty again," Virginia grumbled.

"That's okay," he said. "I'll worsh again. Y'all got plenty of water in that well, ain't 'cha?"

We stood there watching him. Why would anybody wanna pull up weeds?

"These onions are about to suffocate to death," he said. "And you can't find the spring lettuce over there."

Kentucky sighed a big sigh and went to the lettuce bed. She was not dressed for the garden, and her blue cotton dress tail got in her way when she bent over.

Virginia followed slow, and daintily plucked a weed like she was picking lint off of something. Georgia pretended to stump her big toe on a rock. I sat down in the morning glories, whose delicate blue blossoms were beginning to close for the day.

"Did you have to do this for your aunt and uncle?" Georgia said, as she sat down on the ground to examine her wound. Then she reached over beside her, pulled up a radish, and started cleaning the dirt off of it.

"Yeah, but I didn't mind," Tad said. "I always

think of Eugene when I'm weeding. We used to do it together."

"Who?"

"You remember Eugene—Uncle Matthew's boy? It wadn't so bad staying there when he was there. I liked him."

"Oh, yeah, Eugene," Kentucky said. "Did they ever find out what he died of?"

"No, but I know something nobody else knows."

"You do? What?" Kentucky rose up and tucked her dress between her knees.

"Wanna hear 'bout it?" Tad said.

Georgia bit into the radish, and sputtered, "Oo . . . oo, it's pithy!"

"Radishes get pithy when they don't get enough rain," Tad spoke like an old farmer.

"Tell us about Eugene," I reminded him.

"Well, Eugene and me, we were the same age," Tad began, "and when I would go there, we shared a bedroom. He always seemed glad to see me, and I loved to hear him talk. He would tell me some in'eresting stuff."

I noticed that Tad didn't even lose his breath as he talked and weeded at the same time. Kentucky was chugging along, sweating and breathing hard, but almost keeping up with the amount of work he did.

"Eugene was not a happy boy," Tad went on. "I think God sent him to the wrong family. Reckon God makes mistakes like that?"

Tad stood up, his face a question mark.

I coulda said, "Yeah, he does, he sent me to the wrong family, too. Everybody in this family but me's got something special."

But I didn't say anything out loud.

"Anyhow," Tad went on, as he bent again to his work, "Eugene loved animals. It just about broke his heart when a hog or a cow had to be slaughtered, and he wanted a dog so bad he couldn't hardly stand it. He wanted to read, and learn music, and paint pictures, but his mama and daddy told him all them things were a waste of time, and they just made him work, work, work.

"They would say to me and him both, 'Idle hands is the Devil's workshop.'

"But there was this one pretty painting in his room, that Eugene really loved, and when he got a free minute he would set there in front of that pi'ture and study it and listen to it like it was talking to him. He even had a flashlight that he kept beside it to throw light in the shadows.

"That painting had been handed down in Aunt Lucy's family, one generation to another from across the ocean. It was supposed to be famous. It was by some old French feller, maybe a hunert years ago. Anyhow, it was a scene of people all dressed up in their Sunday clothes in a park by a lake. The colors in it were mostly blue, but there was some violet, and a little bit of pink.

"One evening when we were both seven years old, I was laying in the bed, and he was studying the pi'ture, and I ast him, I said, 'Eugene, what'chu lookin' at? You got something treed over there?'

"He laughed and said, 'No, just daydreaming.'

"Then I ast him, 'What do you see in that pi'ture that keeps you all wrapped up in it like that?'

"He said, 'These people are happy. They are doing all the things I wisht I could do.'

"I said, 'Like what?'

"He motioned me to come look over his shoulder at the scene.

" 'Now, study it close,' he said. 'Look at what everybody's doing.'

"So I did. I looked at every person in the pi'ture. Some of them were just strolling along. A boy was playing with a dog. Some people were in boats on the lake. Some were having a picnic. One man was painting a pi'ture, and another one was playing a mandolin and singing. And there was a girl reading a book. But every single one of them was smiling.

"And then Eugene told me that he wanted to be one of them people. And I said yeah, I figgered that would be a right easy life all right.

"A few weeks later I was packing up to go to Uncle Daniel's house for a few months, and Eugene said to me, 'Goodbye, Tadpole, you've been a good friend. The next time you come here, I'll be gone.'

"I ast him, 'Where you goin' to?'

"And he looked over at the pi'ture and said in a soft voice, 'To a happier place.'"

"So he knew he was going to die?" Georgia interrupted, pity dripping from her voice.

"Let me finish," Tad said. "He hugged me goodbye, which was a thing hardly anybody ever did to me—except for Aunt Serilda—after my folks died, so it felt good, and I hugged him back. Then he told me we would meet again someplace else.

"Several months later the kinfolks told me that poor little Eugene had died mysteriously, and nobody knowed what he died of. So when it was time for me to go back to the Birches, I didn't want to go. The first night I just laid in that big empty bedroom by myself, and cried. That's how much I missed him. But you know what?"

"What?"

"I looked over at that pi'ture, and where the moon was shining on it, I thought I saw something."

"What?"

"Well, I got outa bed, and I stood under the pi'ture and looked hard. Then I got Eugene's flashlight, which was still laying there, and I shined it on the scene, and sure enough, there was Eugene, just a'smilin'."

"He was in the PIC-ture?" My voice rose about an octave on the first syllable.

"Sure as the world." Tad went up straight and folded his arms acrost his chest. "That first time I saw him there, he was on one of them boats, and the next day I looked again, and he was having a picnic with some people under a tree. Another time he was painting a pi'ture. Then he was reading a book. Then he was playing the mandolin and singing. Or he was walking the dog. Or just strolling along the water's edge. But every time I looked at that pi'ture he was in it, and he was happy."

There was silence except for the singing of some birds and the katydids playing their summer songs. Then I heard Kentucky chuckling.

"Good one, Tad," came from her. Kentucky caught Virginia's eye, and winked. Then she winked at Georgia, too, and the three of them smiled that I-know-it-all smile. Natur'ly I wadn't included.

"Yeah, that's a good one, Tad," Virginia agreed.

I heard Georgia mumble something that sounded like, "Easter Bunny," and they laughed out loud.

Tad walked over and stood tall above me against the sky. The sun made a halo around his head, and I couldn't see his face. I raised an arm across my for'd to block out some of the glare. He spoke only to me.

"Grownups find it impossible to do what Eugene did."

On the outside I found myself nodding my head up and down, up and down, like a dummy. It was all I could do, but that other me, deep down inside, knowed for certain she was about to hear something important.

Tad knelt beside me, and then I could see his face. "When we're born, we bring magic with us from the other side. One old famous dead poet said we come 'trailing clouds of glory.' Don't you just love that, Carolina—'trailing clouds of glory'?"

His voice was soft, sad, mysterious.

"Yeah," I whispered, wondering why of a sudden his black hair was shinier than it was five minutes ago, and his blue eyes more sparkly.

"When we are little," Tad went on, "we remember the magic, and we use it like Eugene did, and it feels natural. But for some reason, when it's time

to grow up, we think we have to leave the magic behind."

Tad sounded awful growed up his own self.

"But we don't have to?" I crossed my fingers.

"Nope. It's always right in here."

He put one hand on his heart and the other on
mine.

5

AFTER WHILE Tad looked up at the sky, and declared, "It's almost noontime. We got a'right smart done in the garden. Now let's go borry some of McCoy's goats to eat the grass in the yard."

Three goats were fetched, and for the rest of the day Tad stayed busy doing first one thing around the house, and then another. Somehow he managed to drag us into his projects, all the while talking a blue streak so that the whole day working alongside Tad was like one hour at play.

It was my habit at five o'clock every day to walk down to the mouth of the holler to meet Mama's bus. Nobody had ever wanted to go with me before, but this day, when I started out the door, Tad inquired, "Where you going to, Carol?"

And when I told him, he said, "Well, wait up. Let me fire up this here cooking stove for Aunt Serilda, and I'll walk with you."

I couldn't hardly believe it. Was I going to have my cousin all to myself?

That question had barely crossed my mind when Kentucky said, "I wanna go, too."

"Me too," Virginia and Georgia said together.

But we couldn't all go. Somebody had to stay home and keep the goats out of the garden. They were doing a good job mowing the yard, but they would love to get into the real food. So Georgia shrugged and agreed to stay. I knew she didn't mind. It would give her a chance to read. She settled down on the back porch and stuck her nose in her book.

Off we went—Tad, Kentucky, Virginia, and me—and I still couldn't get close to Tad.

When Mama got off the bus, she was carrying a big brown paper poke. I knew they always served fried chicken to the sick people on Sunday, and the kitchen workers were allowed to bring home the leftovers. That's prob'ly what was in the poke.

Mama had T-I-R-E-D wrote all over her, but she still had a smile for us. Right away Tad took her load and carried it for her.

"Fried chicken?" I said to Mama, pointing to the poke.

"No," she said. "For some reason they fixed it

dif'rent today. It's smothered chicken this time, cooked in some herbs. It's kinda runny, so I had to borrow a bowl from the hospital to put it in. Don't let me forget to take it back tomorrow."

We began to walk toward home.

"Aunt Serilda," Tad said with a serious look on his face.

"What is it, Tadpole?"

"You have to call him Tad now," said Virginia. "He's not Tadpole anymore."

Mama just smiled. She reached out and patted his arm lightly, lovingly.

"I wanna ast you an important question, Aunt Serilda," he said, "and you gotta promise you'll give me a straight answer."

"Well, of course." Mama was just as serious as him.

We were all ears. I had to walk backwards in front of him and Mama so I could hear.

"I wanna know how they smothered that chicken? Did they hold a pillow over its face?"

We hee-hawed at that one, even Mama. She had to stop walking and bend over, she was laughing so hard.

"I gotta remember to get that one on Beulah tomorrow," she was able to say at last. "She's the one who smothered it."

With every window open in warm weather, you could hear what was going on in other people's houses as you walked by. That's how everybody in Polly's Fork knew everybody else's business.

But as we walked up the dirt road that Sunday evening in June, we didn't hear anything from the people in the houses along the way, because we were talking and laughing so much our own selves. Folks came out on their porches to listen to us as we walked by, and they got an earful.

"We drew straws at work to see who can be off the Fourth of July, and guess who won?" Mama said.

"Who?" from the four of us.

"I did!" Mama was excited. "I'm going to be off on the Fourth. I wish we could go somewhere. Just to get away. Take a big picnic!"

"Yeah, that would be nice," we mumbled dreamily.

"But we don't have a car," Mama said. "How far can you go without a car?"

Wadn't it the truth?

"Nobody came today?" Mama said to Tad.

"Nobody but Peggy McCoy," he said.

"She ast Tad to come to their house for the Fourth of July," Kentucky said.

"Are you going?" Mama asked him.

"I just had an idea," Tad said. "There's something I wanna talk over with the McCoys, and then I'll let you know."

After we ate that poor smothered chicken, and Mama's warmed-up beans, taters, corn bread, and the other leavin's from yesterday's supper, Mama sat down with Tad, and together they made up a letter.

> *June, 1955*
> *Polly's Fork, Ky.*
>
> *Dear Uncle Matthew and Aunt Lucy:*
> *I want to thank you for all that you done for me, but I was not happy living there at your place, and if it is all the same to you, I do not wish to return. I am sorry if this is inconvenient for you, because for the most part, you have been good to me.*
> *If you have worried about where I was, I am sorry to cause you worry, but I am safe and sound with Aunt Serilda.*
> *Me and her are going to write to the kin and get one of them to take me permanent or temporary either one.*
>
> > *With warmest regards, I remain*
> > *Your devoted and loving nephew,*
> > *Winston Churchill Birch (Tad)*

Then Mama wrote another letter for Tad. He would have to make enough copies to send to each of the relatives on Mama's side of the family. In this letter the situation was explained without saying too much. Tad didn't want to tattle on his uncle and aunt for treating him like a dawg, and besides, he hated pity more'n anybody I ever did see.

The letter just said Tad did not like it at the Birches, and wondered if somebody else in the family would want to keep him permanent, and if not, how about a few months at a time like they used to do? He would work hard for room and board. Mama added a p.s., saying she would love to keep the dear boy her own self, but she simply could not feed and shelter him adequate, circumstances being what they were.

So Tad spent the better part of two hours making copies by hand of Mama's letter. He was real careful not to make any mistakes, and to use his best cursive handwriting skills, like his teachers had learned him.

When he was finished it was nearabout time to go to sleep. Smart Georgia was already curled up with a book in her bed; pretty Virginia was washing her hair in rainwater she had saved in a coffee can; popular Kentucky was coming in the door after taking the goats back home, and visiting with her friend, Leona McCoy; and Carolina the nobody was leafing through one of Mama's books called *The Best of English Verse,* searching for a line by some old famous dead poet about "trailing clouds of glory."

6

THE NEXT DAY was much like the day before. Under Tad's direction we found ourselves accidentally working until Mama came home. Then right after supper Tad walked out into the yard, picking his teeth, and said to me, as I trailed along behind him, "There's nothing like a summer's eve."

You could hear the frogs croaking in the creek, and I was reminded of something.

"Tad, that story 'bout how you got your nickname, is it the truth?"

Tad grinned. "What did you hear?"

"I heard you swallered a tadpole, and then you throwed it back up, and it was still alive."

"That's about the way it was," he said, and took off walking up the road.

"Did you really put it back in the creek?" I called after him.

"Yep! I shore did. Today it's all growed up into a big old bullfrog! The other frogs call him Jonah!"

He had told us earlier that he was going up to see the McCoys on a secret mission, and he didn't want anybody to go with him. It had been dark for two hours when he came back home.

"Where's Aunt Serilda?" he asked as he came in.

"In bed," I said.

Tad perched on the sofa, lifted the window curtain behind it careful, and peeped out.

"Whadda ya looking for out there?" Kentucky asked.

"I'm not sure," he said. "I heard something on the way home."

"The booger man?" Virginia teased.

She was filing and polishing her fingernails.

"Your Uncle Matthew maybe?" I said fearfully.

Tad smiled warmly at me and patted me on the head. "No, Carol. Don't worry about Uncle Matthew going anywhere at night. He's in bed before the sun sets."

"Then what do you think you heard?" Kentucky wanted to know. She was perched on a cushion in a corner, writing a letter to her pen pal in Oregon.

"Well, since it's such a pretty bright night, I decided to take a short cut through that patch of woods below the McCoys'."

"All by yourself?" Georgia poked her nose up over the top of her book.

"I thought so," Tad said. "Only me and the lightning bugs. The air was thick with them, and you could look up and see the tops of the trees swaying against the sky. It was so pretty I took my time. I was deep in the woods when I thought I heard somebody calling my name.

"So I stopped dead still and listened, but I couldn't hear a thang except a rustling of the leaves where the wind was passing through. And I could barely make out the sound of the creek way down yonder, running over the rocks, and the frogs croaking. And somewhere there was a whippoorwill. But nothing else, so I went on.

"And I had not took three steps more when I heard it again. It went like this: 'Win . . . ston . . . Win . . . ston.' "

Tad made his voice sound spooky.

"It did not!" Kentucky said with a laugh. "You're making it up!"

"No I'm not. It called me Winston, which is my real name. Y'all know that."

"It was prob'ly one of them McCoys trying to scare you," Georgia said, yawning and sticking her nose into her book again. She was reading *Jane Eyre* for about the tenth time.

"No it wadn't," Tad said, and he had yet to crack a smile. In fact, he looked solemn as a school-marm. "They don't know my name is Winston."

"So you reckon it was one of us?" Kentucky said, winking at Virginia.

"No, I don't reckon any such'a thang," Tad said. "It was a man's voice. This time I stopped and looked up at the moon, which is still nearly full, and I said, *'What?'* just like that, and lifted my hands to the sky."

"And what did the moon say back?" Virginia couldn't help laughing, I reckon, but it was clear to me that Tad felt put out and put down.

He shrugged, and clammed up.

"You didn't hear your name again?" said I, hoping he would go on with it, in spite of certain people being ugly and making fun of him.

For the second time in as many days, Tad turned and spoke directly to me, ignoring my sisters.

"Yeah, I did."

"Who do you think it was, Tad?"

"I've heard the same voice in a dream I had twice—no, three times now. It was a man calling my name, and he talked to me. When I woke up, I thought I could hear him still."

"And it was the same voice?"

"The very same. The first time I heard it was at Uncle Jake's. It was when he had that big old drafty house with all them rooms to it, remember that house?

"It was in the middle of the day that time, and we were fixin' to go somewhere—I kaint recall where exactly—but the whole family was waiting for me in the truck, and I couldn't find my shoes. I was running around looking under beds and behind doors, and I don't know where all.

"And I heard that voice, 'Win . . . ston . . . Win . . . ston.'

"I stopped and stood perfectly still, and listened. I knowed I was in the house by myself 'cause through the window I could see Uncle Jake and Aunt Nancy out there in the cab of the truck with the baby, and the other young'uns were in the back.

"And I heard it again, 'Win . . . ston . . . Win . . . ston.'

"That time I whispered, 'Who is it?'

"And you know what that voice said to me?"

I could only shake my head, unable to fathom what was coming next.

"It whispered right in my ear, 'You know me.' "

My sisters, in spite of their proud ways, and making fun of Eugene going into the picture and all, had plum forgot what they were doing, and set there with their mouths hanging open.

"When I found my shoes, I went on outside," Tad continued. "And I climbed into the truck bed with my cousins, and Uncle Jake started the engine. As we were pulling away, I glanced back at the house, and up on the second floor where I had been, I saw a man standing in the window looking out at me."

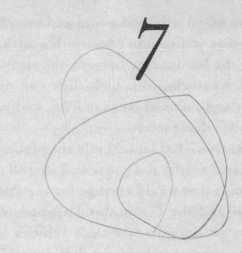

7

BY AND BY, Tad broke the magic spell by standing up and grinning a big grin at the four of us scattered around the room.

"I cooked up a surprise for Aunt Serilda. We're going on a picnic to the Breaks on the Fourth of July."

"The Breaks!" from all of us.

"How?" from Kentucky.

Almost two centuries ago, the legendary Daniel Boone, his own self, had explored the Breaks of the Cumberland, which was only a few miles over the mountains from Polly's Fork. Last year it had been made into the first public park in our part of the world, to be enjoyed by all and sundry.

So far, none of us had been lucky enough to

visit it, but we heard tell it was a wild and beautiful place with a view you couldn't beat with a stick. It was right on the border line between the states of Virginia and Kentucky, with high cliffs and deep gorges, miles and miles of trails to hike, and picnic tables under shade trees.

"It was like this," Tad said. "I told the McCoys I would be pleased to play the guitar and sing all day long for them if they would arrange for the Pughs and the Mills and the Cottons and anybody else who wants to go along to take their vehicles and find a place to squeeze in my Aunt Serilda and her four girls, and me too, natur'ly."

Again mouths fell open. In the short time he'd been with us, he'd managed to organize a neighborhood picnic—with music—to the Breaks, which everybody would be dying to go to.

"I kinda suggested Mrs. McCoy be in charge of planning the day," Tad went on. "Just to get her excited, you know. She usta be a schoolteacher before she had a house full of young'uns, and you know how teachers are about planning and organizing. She started taking over before I had the words out of my mouth.

"She said we should go in the afternoon, and first we'll sing some patriotic songs to celebrate our country's birthday. Then she reckoned we orta do some gospel singing to thank the Lord for our freedom and plenty. Then we'll have dinner on the ground.

"After we eat, she figures we'll be ready to rest a spell or go exploring or hiking or playing games with the kids. Then around dark we'll come back together and eat some more. There are lights out there after dark. The state pays for 'em.

"She said she's going to see the Pughs in the morning, Leona is going to the Mills, and Clementine to the Cottons. They said if any of them don't want to go, they'll round up somebody else with vehicles to make sure we have room a'plenty for everybody."

"Tad, do you think you can get that many people in Polly's Fork to agree on something?" Kentucky said.

"I shore do," Tad said. "Specially since I promised a square dance."

"A square dance!" Virginia hooted. "Can you call a square dance, Tad?"

"Is the world round?"

"But you can't do it without a fiddle!" Georgia declared.

"And who says I don't got a fiddle?"

"You do?"

"Mr. McCoy says the Boultons have one that nobody plays, and he's pretty sure I can borry it."

"But can you play it?" I said.

"Course I can!" he cried, with another big grin. "Uncle Warner learned me one time!"

For the first time, prob'ly ever, them loud-mouthed Collins gals were speechless.

"And by the way, Ken," Tad went on, "Mrs. McCoy put you in charge of keeping a list of the goings-on."

"Meaning . . . ?" from Kentucky.

"Meaning once we get the go-ahead from the neighbors, you keep a list of what food everybody's fixin', and who's riding with who, that kind of thing. You gotta be specially nice to the Pughs. Remember they got candy and pop and stuff in their grocery store. You git my meanin'?"

Then there was such an explosion of excited twittering and chirping among us that Mama woke up and came out of the bedroom in her robe. When she heard what was going on, she clapped her hands like a little girl. I had never seen her do that before.

Tad and Kentucky spent the next day visiting neighbors, and finding out who wanted to be included in the picnic. The Cottons couldn't go, and they were awful disappointed, but they had already promised their kin over in Grundy to come to their house on the Fourth. But the Hatfield family and the Boultons wanted to be included.

Kentucky wrote down what each family was

planning to bring, just to make sure we didn't wind up with five batches of tater salad and nothing to drink. She also had a list of what vehicles everybody had, and how many people you could cram in them. The McCoys had a pickup truck and a car both, but everybody else had trucks, which was good, 'cause you could haul a lot of people in the back of a pickup—barring rain.

Tad borrowed the Boultons' fiddle, which he bowed and plucked till his neck got sore. He didn't sound bad either.

After supper that evening the six McCoy girls, ages nine to seventeen, came down to talk about the big day coming up. They were chatterboxes.

Kentucky brung the radio out on the porch and turned it up loud, and everybody started dancing in the road. I wadn't much for dancing, so I stayed on the porch, listened close to the music, and hummed along in a low voice.

Suddenly Tad was beside me, humming with me.

"You hear the layers, don't you?" he asked after a while.

"The what?"

"The layers of music. You can hear another line of notes running underneath the melody, can't you? That's what you're humming."

"Yeah!" I said, surprised that he knew what I was doing. "Do you hear it, too?"

"Shore I hear it," Tad said with a smile. "It's called harmony."

"I been hearing it since I was a little girl," I said. "But just lately I been trying to sing it. Some songs are easier than others."

"You've got a good ear, Carol."

Then Leona McCoy grabbed him away from me, and he went dancing off with her. I noticed that his shoe soles were flapping as he danced.

Later, when the household was asleep, I lay in bed beside Mama, listening to the songs in my head. Gradually they blended with the babbling of the creek and the rustling of the leaves, the croaking of the frogs and the singing of the whippoorwill, until a whole orchestra was out there in those wild dark hills, harmonizing with me.

8

BY THURSDAY MORNING Tad was a bundle of nerves. Eight or ten cars passed on the road before noon, and each time Tad froze at whatever he was doing, and listened.

At noon Kentucky and Virginia ate a hasty lunch and took off to visit the McCoys, while Tad and me and Georgia lingered over our cold beans and taters.

"Tad, why you so nervous?" I asked.

"Uncle Matthew prob'ly got my letter yesterday, or he'll git it today. Now he knows for sure where I'm at."

"But you told him you didn't want to stay with him. Do you still expect he'll come for you?"

Tad laughed. "What I want makes no difference to him!"

I was wondering why you would want a person in your house who didn't care to be there, when Tad spoke again soft, "Uncle Matthew looks at me and sees nothing but free labor."

I laid one hand on his arm. "Don't you worry, Tad. I'm pretty good with engine noises. I'll let you know whan I hear a strange one."

"That's the truth," Georgia agreed. "Everybody who lives up the holler from us, and has to pass our house, Carol knows the sound of their car."

"That's a rare talent," Tad said. "What do you do when somebody gits a new car?"

I shrugged. "I never knowed anybody to git a new car."

In the next half hour three vehicles passed our house. Each time Tad paused at what he was doing to look at me.

The first two times I listened and said, "Wrong direction." The third one I recognized as a truck, but I couldn't tell whose it was. It was traveling from the mouth of the holler, which was the way Tad's Uncle Matthew would have to come.

I hollered, "Git down!" and the three of us hit the floor. The front door and windows were open, and we didn't want to be seen.

The strange truck stopped out front.

"To the back room!" Georgia whispered loud. "Under the bed!"

We scuttled on our hands and knees through the kitchen and into the back bedroom, where Georgia rolled under one bed and Tad under the other. I followed Tad. He had his spine to the wall, and I scrunched up close to him, with my back against his chest.

There was a sound at the front of the house. You couldn't call it a knock. It was more like a banging and rattling of the screen door.

"Hey! Y'all home?" somebody growled loud, and Tad took in a sharp breath.

"It's him," he whispered.

The banging came again, and then we heard the door open and close as Matthew Birch entered the house. I could feel Tad breathing into my hair, and I laid a light hand over my mouth to keep my own breath quiet. We heard Matthew's footsteps in the living room and front bedroom. Then he moved into the kitchen.

"Hello!" His voice boomed throughout the house.

The only answer he got was from a gathering of orioles chirping outside the bedroom window.

From where I lay I could see the curtain that separated the kitchen from the back bedroom being lifted. Then I saw heavy black boots. They were scuffed up bad and had dried mud caked on them. Or maybe that was not mud at all. I smelled manure.

Matthew Birch took a few steps into the room and stood there as the curtain fell back into place behind him. I could feel Tad's heart pounding against my back, and I thought my own heart was gonna explode for sure.

The way the bed covers hung almost to the floor, I could not see Georgia at all, but I couldn't hear her breath, so I figgered Matthew Birch couldn't hear ours either.

Then the boots turned around as the man in them mumbled with disgust, something that sounded like, "Beatchallpeepuddin." It's no tellin' what he really said. And he stomped out of the house. Still we didn't move until we heard the engine start up. I could tell he was turning around in the middle of the road.

Tad let out his breath in a great gust of relief as the sound of the motor moved down the holler. "That was a close call, Carol. Shore glad you know them engine sounds like you do."

"I'll know his next time," I assured him. "I could tell it was a truck."

"That's right," Tad said. "It's a forty-nine Ford."

We scooted out into the floor between the

two beds. Georgia's cheeks looked like two crab apples.

"I'm just a'shakin'," she said, and held out one hand for us to see.

Tad laughed as he stood up and dusted off his britches.

"Shucks! Don't let Uncle Matthew rattle you. He's skeered his own self. He has to act big to cover it up."

A few days later I walked down to the mouth of the holler with Tad to the post office. He was hoping to hear from one of the relatives who might want to take him in, but all he got was a letter from Lucy Birch, Matthew's wife.

> *Tadpole, boy, you come on home now and hep yer Uncle you know I got the gout real bad and ant much hep to him my own sef. He wont beet you if yul just mind him, and not sass.*
>
> *yours in jesus Lucy Birch*

"What's the gout?" I asked Tad as I read over his shoulder.

"Her feet git swolled up big," Tad said.

"You gonna go?" I said.

Tad folded the letter up and placed it in his pocket. Then he picked up a rock and threw it over the Polly's Fork bridge into the river before answering me.

"Not unless I have to."

In the days following, we were busily planning for our picnic at the Breaks. We heard no more from the Birches, nor from the relatives, and for the time being we placed them uneasily on a shelf in the back of our minds.

9

THE FOURTH OF JULY dawned bright and clear, a beautiful warm day. The entire household was up and about earlier than usual, and as jittery as hummingbirds.

Mama commenced cooking right away. She was fixing blackberry dumplings and roastin' ears, lots of other vegetables from our garden, and buttermilk biscuits.

Kentucky, the social butterfly, took off on winged sandals to go from house to house and check on everybody who was going.

Virginia, the peacock, was laying out what she was going to wear. Lavender and pink were "in" that summer, so she had dyed her old white shorts lavender. She already had a pink halter.

Georgia, the bookworm, was reading aloud to anybody who would listen, about the adoption of the Declaration of Independence on July 4, 1776.

And I was Tad's shadow. He was practicing some old-timey gospel hymns, then patriotic songs, then bluegrass, then folk. I knew them ever' one, and I was right at his elbow, trying to find the harmony under the surface of the tunes he played. He didn't seem to mind me.

He wrote down a long list of songs in a tablet he got from Mama, and after while, he also wrote down some square dance calls. Just so he didn't forget, he said. He confided in me that he had never really called a square dance before, but he had seen a few, and had memorized everything.

The Pughs, who owned a grocery store up the holler a piece from us, come by in their pickup for me and Tad and Mama. They had closed up shop for the day, and brung pokes full of goodies. The other girls were to follow with the Boultons.

Mama had her food packed in a dishpan full of ice. Mr. Pugh got out of the cab of the truck and put her stuff in the back with me and Tad, the two Pugh boys, Roger and Doug, and three of the McCoy girls. Mama got up in the cab with Mr. and Mrs. Pugh. Everybody was in a playful mood as we took off down the road, leaving a trail of dust behind.

We rode to the highway and traveled it for about twenty minutes before we started winding up a hairpin road that curled around the mountainside to the Breaks. You could look down far below and see the road you had just been on.

"These curves are so sharp," Tad said, "you could just about ketch your own tail."

The McCoy girls giggled at everything Tad said, like he was Jerry Lewis or somebody.

There were lots of other people already there at the Breaks, but it was a sizable place, and we soon found a spot near a creek that we thought was big enough for our crowd. Mr. Pugh said we could pull four picnic tables together, and he got Tad, Doug, and Roger to help him do that.

The Boultons arrived with their children and my sisters, and everybody else was there in a while. The air was electrified with celebration. Tad started performing almost before the hellos were out of the way. He went strolling amongst our neighbors with his guitar, flashing his dazzling smile, and singing to them:

> *Why don't you haul off and love me one more time?*
> *Why don't you squeeze me until I'm turning blind?*
> *If you don't cuddle up and love me, like I want you*
>   *to do,*
> *I'm gonna haul off and die over you!*

Some of the girls already were dancing on the grass. The boys, in their overalls, were hanging back and watching with bashful grins, hands in pockets.

The women were laying out food on the picnic tables, and fussing about this or that, purely from habit, but good-naturedly on this day. The men were loafing under the trees by the creek, smoking and cracking jokes.

The younger children were starting up games of Round Town and Red Rover. Yesterday I woulda been right in there with them, playing games, but today I was a barefooted dancer on the green.

"Patriotic now!" Mrs. McCoy was hollering at Tad, and clapping her hands sharply. "Let's not forget to honor our country!"

"How about the 'Star-Sprinkled Banana'?" someone hollered, and Tad went right into the national anthem before Mrs. McCoy had time to react to that disrespectful title. Everybody stood at attention and tried to sing along.

After that one, we sung "America the Beautiful," "God Bless America," and "The Battle Hymn of the Republic." Then nobody could think of another patriotic American song, so we did "My Old Kentucky Home."

Weep no more, my lady,
Oh weep no more today.

We will sing one song
For the old Kentucky home,
For the old Kentucky home far away.

After we sung praises to the Lord, dinner was ready, and Calvin McCoy blurted out a blessing right off the top of his head.

Lord, we thank you for what we've got.
If there's more in the pot, bring it on while it's hot!

Before he could duck, his mama had done wopped him up the side of his head with the palm of her hand, but that did not stop everybody from laughing, including Calvin and Mrs. McCoy. Then she did her own more suitable blessing, and the feast commenced.

There was fried chicken and baked ham, taters fixed five different ways, and about ten other kinds of vegetables, salads, watermelon and muskmelon, all kinds of bread and real butter, cakes, pies, and cold drinks a'plenty. All four picnic tables were covered with food, and people were spreading blankets on the ground to take their plates to and eat.

My strategy was to take one spoonful of each dish, as I wanted to taste everything. My plate was spilling over when I set down with Mama and Tad and my sisters. Around us the other families were settling down to eat with their children, who ranged in age from three months to seventeen years.

Amy Hatfield, who was eighteen, and no longer considered one of the children, sat near us with her intended. He was a good-looking sailor from Riverbend, named Ron Keith something-or-other. He had helped us out by bringing his daddy's Jeep and hauling some of the kids.

With dreamy eyes, the girls watched the sailor in his crisp white uniform, while the eyes of the boys, like slaves, followed Amy. She had a waistline about the size of a broomstick, and a corn-silk ponytail.

A few minutes into the meal a quietness settled over us, and I knew this eating business had got serious.

Gradually the talk started up again. First it was coal mining, and how it was going to the dawgs since the Yankees barged in and started stripping the tops off the mountains.

"Reckon we orta go up North and do the same for them," Mr. Boulton remarked. "See how they like it."

"I had a cousin from Blackberry Fork went up North," somebody spoke, and when I glanced around, I saw that it was Mrs. Mills. I hardly recognized her, since she used to be real big and fat, but she had fell off a lot. "He wrote me that he makes better wages there for half the labor he done here."

"Same with my brother," Mr. Hatfield said. "They make some good money up there."

"My husband wanted us to move up there one time," Mama chimed in. "It was when we were living at that coal camp over near Hazard. Remember when they had that camp there? Well, that's where we lived then, and anyhow, he said they had mining camps up North where the living conditions were better than these down here. For one thing, they had bathrooms."

"I'm surprised you didn't do that," Mrs. Pugh said. "Why didn't you?"

Mama hesitated. "Well, if you wanna know the plain old truth of it," she fessed up at last, "I didn't want a child named Pennsylvania!"

If we'd been in a house right then, my mama woulda brung it down. You never heard such guffawing in your life. I was downright impressed. For a quiet person, she'd done good.

Then Mr. Hatfield drawed our attention to the fact that the Hatfields and McCoys were sitting side by side, peaceably eating dinner on the ground together.

The famous bloody feud between the Hatfields and McCoys had actually happened in our corner of the world. It was not something we had to study in school. We growed up knowing about it from our kin.

Now there were Hatfields and McCoys all over Kentucky and West Virginia, being good neighbors. Some of them had even married each other and borned babies together.

There was talk about the drought we'd just passed through.

"If it hadn't a' rained when it did," Mr. McCoy said, "I'd a' had to plow my garden under and plant cactuses."

Next followed the most favorite discussion of all for grownups, and that was their young'uns.

They carried on about who had give up the bottle and started eating solid food, who had finally got shed of pinworms, who quit wetting in the bed, or quit stuttering or sucking their thumb.

For the bigger kids they bragged about who had passed a grade, got a sweetheart, got baptized, learned to drive, made the glee club, plowed his first plot, or plaited her own hair.

Everybody was complimenting and congratulating everybody else on their young'uns, and somebody said to Mama, "I'll tell you one thang right now, Serilda Collins, that Tadpole's one fine boy."

"We think so," Mama responded, beaming at Tad and ruffling his curls fondly.

"It's Tad," Tadpole said, blushing and grinning. "Y'all call me Tad. That's my new name."

"Them's some fine gals you got there, too. You can be proud."

"I am," Mama agreed, and smiled around at us.

Somebody said, "I never seed a girl as young as your Kentucky talk like she does to any old body about any old thang. Never meets a stranger, that girl. I just love to see her coming up the road."

Kentucky beamed.

Said another, "And you'll have to keep Virginia locked up when she gets big enough to court, or git you a shotgun!"

Virginia glowed.

Still another said, "A certain teacher told me one day that Georgia Collins is the best student she ever had the pleasure to teach."

Georgia pursed her lips and tried not to smile.

Silence fell. I knowed things were heading this way, for hadn't I been through it in my mind a thousand times? Didn't they know they were setting me up for this pure-tee mortification?

While everybody was searching their brains for something good to say about me, Peggy McCoy had to open her big mouth. With blackberry dumplings dripping off her dimpled face, she giggled and sputtered, "Carol's just a runt, ain't she? Y'all kaint brag on her."

"Who pulled your chain?" I spit out hotly, and drawed a smattering of laughs.

In the back of my mind a movie was running, and in it I was slowly torturing Peggy—with rats and waspers, catypillars, black racer snakes, maybe a bat or two.

Kentucky spoke up. "Why, Carol's the sweetest one in our family."

"She's my baby," Mama said warmly, and patted my skinny legs.

"She certainly is a sweet little thang," the neighbors agreed quick enough.

What made them think that would make me feel better? Who wants to be a sweet little thang? Who wants to be the baby?

Then I was aware of Tad's eyes on me.

"You mark my words." He was being kind. "Carolina Collins is gonna surprise everybody one of these days. Just you wait and see."

Followed by comments like, "That's right," or "Shore as the world."

But I was not comforted.

One of these days? Wait and see?

What about *now*? Wadn't there one thing about me now that folks could brag about? Not one little bitty thing? When the talk went on to something else, I stuck my tongue out at Peggy.

With dinner winding down, Mr. Pugh started

passing around big red wax lips which he had brung from his store, for the young'uns. The other children took their lips, put them in place, and started prancing around the tables, acting silly. I set my wax lips aside and pushed chocolate cake around on my plate. I had been looking forward to finishing off my dinner with this piece of cake, and now it tasted like mud.

10

WHEN EVERYBODY was miserable from eating too much, the rest of the food was wrapped and placed in tubs, which were set in the cold creek water. The leftover ice was packed around the food.

"It'll save until supper," the women said, "but then, warm as it is, we'll have to finish it off, or throw it away."

The afternoon was a whirlwind of games; playing in the creek; more singing; listening to jokes I didn't understand; picking berries along the many trails; leaning over the guardrails at the scenic overlooks just to scare the fool out of the grownups; and finally, near dark, the shifting of the food from the the creek back to the picnic tables for another feast.

Then it was square dance time! Tad was already warming up beneath a tree by the creek. Everybody was chomping at the bit to get started. Some were in the shadows, going over their steps.

I wanted to square-dance, but I was afraid I might be out of place, so I wandered over to where the young'uns were sitting in a circle around the dance area, feeling like I didn't belong there either.

Barefooted, with mulberry stains on our fingers and little rings of dirt around our necks, where we had sweated, we were sucking suckers, swatting gnats, and scratching ourselves. It looked like we might be taking home some poison ivy, chiggers on our butts, and prob'ly a tick or two apiece.

Then there was Tad, striking up a stance with the fiddle, and hollerin' out, "Claim your partner!"

Ron Keith and Amy leapt out in the middle first. I could see that Amy, being fair-complected, had sunburned herself, but that didn't slow her down a bit.

After them, here come Kentucky dragging Calvin McCoy behind her, both of them red in the face. He acted like he was trying to get away, but he was grinning and not trying too hard. Next Beau Hatfield grabbed Clementine McCoy, and the plump but pleasant Mills twins, who had been so quiet I nearly forgot about them, paired up with Virginia and Georgia.

All the young people, from about eleven up, followed in a bunch. Everybody found a partner. Last came the family men with their wives.

It was then I thought of Mama. I looked for her, and there she was sitting on the ground by herself, watching the square dance unfold before her. She kept a smile pasted on her face, but I could see that she was not smiling inside. She was thinking the same thing I was—that she had no partner.

Could it be that she felt lonely and left out?

To consider Mama's feelings was a whole new way of thinking for me. But after that first thought, others came in a flood. For instance, what did she think of when she saw women riding by in cars with their husbands? Did she wish she had a man with a car to drive her places? And when she heard love songs like "Blue Moon of Kentucky," did it remind her of Daddy and how he had left her alone?

The saddest part was that she was the youngest-looking and the prettiest woman there. That had never occurred to me before either—my mama was real pretty! It was plain to see where Virginia got her good looks.

"Swing your partner!" from Tad, and the dance went into first gear.

I saw Mama start to clap her hands, so I did, too, and soon everybody was clapping. Tad did a real good job. He hollered out all the calls loud and clear.

The dance went into second gear: "Spin the top round and round."

Then third: "And a dosie-doe!"

Fourth! "Pass on through."

Reverse! "Reverse the flutter!"

"Change your partner!"

The first dance ended with a huge round of applause for Tad, a lot of laughter, and excited chatter. The second dance went about the same as the first. A few people tried to buck-dance, but they soon found out they couldn't do it on the grass. You gotta have a hard surface for buck-dancing.

On the third dance there was some shifting around of partners, and after that nearly everybody danced, including me and the other kids, even Mama. Each man there respectfully asked her to dance, but none of them more than once.

Mama's cheeks became flushed with the unusual activity, and her eyes were shiny, so that she looked even prettier than ever. But after a while, she was all alone again, and I went to sit with her.

I think it was about eleven o'clock when I fell asleep with my head on Mama's lap. When she woke me up, people were loading up the vehicles to go home. I climbed in beside Tad, feeling about as grungy and grumpy as an old sow.

Mr. Pugh drove careful down the mountain. You could see his yellow headlight beams cutting through the pitch-black night, around the lonely hairpin curves. Tad sat with his head against the back of the cab, perfectly quiet. I figured he must be awful tired, too. The other children in the back of the truck were sprawled over each other, fast asleep.

Watching the tops of the trees against the night sky, I was reminded of the voice Tad had told us about.

"You give out, Tad?" I asked him.

"I feel like an old horse that's been rode hard and put up wet," he came back sluggishly, giving me a sideways smile. Then he closed his eyes.

"Can I ast you something, Tad?"

"Hmm," was all he said.

"About that voice you heard in the woods?"

"Hmm?"

"And in your dreams, and in Uncle Jake's house, and then you saw him standing in that window."

"Hmm?"

"Was it your daddy?"

"My daddy?" He sat up then and looked at me. "You know my daddy's dead. Why'd you ast me that?"

"Well, he whispered in your ear that you knew him, so I figured . . ."

"His ghost, you mean? No, not my daddy's ghost, but it *is* somebody who wants to help me."

"You got any idea who he is, Tad?"

"Yeah, I got an idea it's *me*, little Carol, it's me all growed up. He comes to me through time and space to look after me, and help me in hard times."

For a moment I felt like I had to ration my breath to keep it from gittin' away from me.

"*A visit from the future?*" I panted, but Tad had done settled back on the cab, and closed his eyes again, like we'd been discussing something as ordinary as weather.

After a long time I thought he might be asleep, and I ventured a whisper to the treetops.

"Can I have a visit like that, too?"

"I don't think so, Carol," Tad spoke up promptly. "I think he comes to me 'cause I got no parents. I have nobody to help me grow up. But you got Aunt Serilda. You have the best mama in the world, and don't you ever forget it."

11

IT WAS SO DARK when we got home from the Breaks nobody saw the note tacked to the front screen door. Mama discovered it as she left for work the next morning.

> *Tadpole Birch this makes twist I come to git you and you waz gone. It's a waist of gass, that's what it is. Next time you better be here the law says you belong to me*
>
> *Uncle Matthew Birch*

She handed it to Tad on his couch, and we clustered around him. As he read, we saw something pass over his face like the shadow of a cloud moving over the earth.

" 'You belong to me'!" Mama quoted Matthew

Birch, spitting the words out of her mouth with distaste. "Like you're one of his farm animals, or . . . or a stick of furniture!"

"But, Aunt Serilda, the law says—"

"Hang the law!" Mama interrupted him, and I was surprised. It was not like her one little bit to go against the law. "You don't have to go!"

She started out the door again, but turned back to him, and her face was red as a cherry. "If they come while I'm at work, you run, you heah me, Tad? You run up to the McCoys' or somebody else's place. You tell them what's going on. They'll hide you. You tell them how your uncle beat you with a horsewhip!"

I heard my sisters gasp.

"Sh . . . shh!" Tad glanced around at us.

"I know I promised you not to tell, Tadpole, but I can't help it. I'm mad and I don't care who knows it!"

I had never seen my mama like this. "I understand you don't want folks thinking bad of your daddy's brother, and feeling sorry for you, but there's no sense in a man beatin' a boy. There's no sense in it, and I won't have it!"

Mama stomped out then and hurried down the road to catch her bus.

"With a horsewhip?" Georgia managed to say at last, her eyes filled with tears.

Virginia and Kentucky stood with their heads bowed like they were at church.

I had never seen a horsewhip, but the way my sisters were carrying on, it must be a hideous thing. It was plain, by its name, that it was a whip you beat a horse with, and that in itself seemed like an evil thing to do, even to an animal.

"So what?" Tad brushed it away crankily. "Could y'all go on now and let a feller git his clothes on?"

Slowly the four of us walked into the kitchen and gathered around the table without a word. Mama had stewed blackberries with butter, and fixed biscuits stuffed with thick slabs of side meat. In a few minutes Tad came in and poured a cup of coffee from the stove. As was his habit, he tipped the coffee into his saucer to cool, and sipped it slow.

Georgia was filling his plate for him, and Virginia fetched the molasses, pouring it over his side-meat biscuit, just the way he liked it.

He took note of what was being done for him.

"It didn't hurt anyhow," he said after a while, and tried to eat his breakfast, but I reckon he had lost his appetite.

After cleaning up the kitchen, me and Tad and Kentucky walked down to the Polly's Fork post office, but again there was no mail from anybody.

It looked like the kin did not want to be bothered with Tad.

In the afternoon we went far into the hills to pick blackberries, and while we were gone, another note was left on the front porch. This one was attached to a shoe box. Inside was a pair of men's wing-tipped shoes, size eight. The note read:

Can't wear no more too little maybe Tadpole can wear

Mr. Pugh

Tad was tickled. He tried the shoes on. Perfect fit. He strutted on the porch for a few turns, then placed them careful back in the box.

"I'll save 'em for going places," he said.

Georgia studied the box the shoes came in. "These shoes ain't second-handed, Tad. They're brand-new from Mr. Pugh's store."

Virginia smiled as she ran her hand over the soft black leather. "Wadn't that good of him?" She loved nice things.

We had picked three buckets full of berries, which we took into the house and set on the kitchen table. We reckoned Mama would can them when she got home from work, like she always did, but Tad had other ideas.

"Kaint just about anybody can blackberries?" he said. "How hard could it be?"

Georgia grunted irritably and picked up her book. Virginia went to turn on the rotating fan, which, at that moment, was set on a corner shelf to cool the kitchen, but nothing happened.

"Hmm," she mused. "Something's wrong with the fan."

I opened the refrigerator to get some ice, and found it dark inside.

"Something's wrong with the Frigidaire, too," I said.

Kentucky checked the radio. Nothing happened.

Me and my sisters all knew at the same time.

"Oh, no, I betcha the power company's been here and turned off the juice!"

"Why would they do that?" Tad wanted to know.

Nobody answered him. We didn't know for absolute sure right then, but we had a sneaky suspicion that we had traded our electricity for two hours of looking at James Dean. Kentucky and Virginia walked out on the back porch. Me and Georgia set down at the kitchen table.

Tad went to start up a fire in the backyard. He placed our big black pot over it, and drawed up enough water from the well to sterilize the Mason jars. While the water was coming to a boil, he pulled the jars and lids out from under the porch, where they were stored. Grumpy and silent, my sisters fell into helping him.

I didn't walk to meet Mama that evening. I didn't want to face her. When she came in, wore out as always, I was glad the blackberries were canned and lined up on shelves in the back bedroom.

"Having you here, Tad, is a blessing," she told him. "You're a good influence on my girls."

She went to the Frigidaire and started to pull things out to fix for supper.

"How come there's no light in here?" Mama touched the walls of the refrigerator. "And it's all sweaty inside."

Nobody answered her. I noticed that Tad stood with his back against the wall, one foot propped up behind him. With arms crossed, he watched us all like we were fuzzy-headed critters he was studying for a science lesson. Still nobody else said anything. We could not look each other in the eye.

You could see the truth dawning on Mama's face as she pulled the light cord over the table and nothing happened.

"Oh, I see," she said, and sank down heavily in a cane-bottomed chair.

"I guess the power company come while we were out picking blackberries," I said.

"Kaint you pay the bill?" Kentucky had the nerve to ask her.

Mama's face went red for the second time that day. "Y'all told me the bills would get paid somehow, remember? You said they always git paid. Didn't you say that?"

She glared at us, and we had no answer for her. Mama had always took care of things. Couldn't she manage this, too?

"Oh, I know you're just kids." Mama gave a weighty sigh, and rested her cheek on one hand. "And I shouldn't a' listened to you."

We all went into private, dark thoughts for a long time.

"I paid part of the bill on payday, but we were two months behind," she finally explained.

She acted like she was apologizing to us, when we were the ones who orta be doing that.

"I thought the power company would give me a little more time. I don't know why I thought that. They want their money just like everybody else."

Tad took the seat beside Mama at the table. All of her sadness was reflected in his eyes.

"We had no electricity up on that mountain when I was growing up," Mama recalled. "We had no Frigidaire, no electric lights, no radio, no fan. And it wadn't so bad."

"But we kaint listen to the radio," I said. (Maybe I whined.)

"And we kaint read after dark," Georgia complained.

"It's so hot without the fan," Virginia moaned.

"Our food will spoil," Kentucky added.

Tad watched and listened in silence.

"What're we gonna do?" we all appealed to Mama.

"I don't know what *y'all* are gonna do," Mama said, now disgusted with her girls, who only yesterday she had said she was proud of. "You can figger things out for a change!"

We were startled.

"I'm tired," she murmured, and I felt my pulse fluttering like a little bird. Hadn't she said that was the reason our daddy left us those years ago? He was tired, too.

"I wash my hands of it right now," she went on. "If you want electricity, you'll find a way to pay the bill!"

12

DURING SUMMER it didn't get dark until nearly nine o'clock anyhow, so that night nobody but Georgia missed the electric lights that much. It was the radio that I missed.

When Mama went to bed, Georgia went, too. Tad took his guitar out on the front porch, and set there in the dark, picking and singing low and slow, so he wouldn't disturb Mama. In some places I practiced harmony, and Tad helped me. Kentucky and Virginia sat nearby, quiet for once, and didn't join in.

The next morning Tad was up before Mama. I heard him fire up the stove for her, and they talked low while she fixed breakfast. The two of them had already dressed and finished eating when the rest of us got up. Tad had on clean clothes, and his new shoes.

"Now, Ken and Gin"—Mama started with her daily instructions—"I want y'all to pick them green beans out there today. The vines are loaded down, and we're gonna have to can 'em, or they'll go to the bad."

Groans from Ken and Gin.

"Georgia, you gather the other vegetables before the sun gets too hot, or they'll wilt on the vine, you heah me?"

Georgia grunted.

"And, Carol, try to—"

"I know!" I snapped, surprising my own self more than anybody else. "Stay out of the way!"

Mama kissed me and said no more.

She didn't give instructions to Tad that day, and we soon found out why. When she went out the door, he went with her.

"Where you goin' to?" I hollered after him.

"To work!" he hollered back over his shoulder, as the two of them went down the road.

I watched them disappear around the bend, and wondered why I was so dadblamed mad. We ate breakfast in grumpy silence.

Georgia went to the garden while it was still wet with dew, and gathered onions, tomatoes, radishes, cucumbers, peppers, and corn, like

Mama told her to do. She also found one ripe muskmelon, but all the spring lettuce, which was my favorite, had done dried up and blowed away.

She come in and dumped everything on the table, picked up a book of short stories by Edgar Allan Poe, and escaped from the rest of us, into another world.

Kentucky and Virginia put off going to the garden as long as they could, and when they finally did go, the sun was so high they like to died of heatstroke. They hollered for me to bring them water about once every fifteen minutes.

I didn't fuss about it, 'cause at least they were not telling me to stay out of the way. After while, between water runs, I set down amongst the bowing sunflowers that edged the garden, plucked out their seeds, and ate them.

When the beans were picked, Kentucky and Virginia were sunburned. They went inside, dumped the beans on the table, and dunked their faces in cold well water.

It was a depressing afternoon, and so hot in the house we felt like we were being baked in a box. Me and Georgia went out and set ourselves down in the creek for a while. Kentucky and Virginia were too proud to do such a childish thing, so they stayed miserable.

When Tad came home around four o'clock, we

were in the kitchen, eating tomatoes and cucumbers with salt. Tad looked at the beans and other vegetables on the kitchen table. Everybody had done what they were told to do, but no more.

"Did you find a job?" Kentucky asked, and handed him a salted tomato.

"Yeah," Tad answered her, ate the tomato in two bites, and went for another one.

"Doin' what?" Virginia wanted to know.

"This and that," was all he said as he downed two whole jelly glasses full of water.

Then Tad set down at the table and started stringing beans. Kentucky went out on the back porch, slamming the screen door behind her, like she had been insulted. Virginia followed. Georgia returned to the living room to read her book.

I stayed with Tad.

He smiled at me. "Do I stink, or something?"

I smiled back and shook my head. Then an original thought somehow found its way into my head. Why not *volunteer* to help Tad string beans? I wondered where did such a confounded idea come from?

I picked up a bean and looked at it. I watched Tad. Yeah, zip, zip, and snap, snap, snap just the way Mama did it. I joined him without a word. He smiled at me again.

"What kind of work did you find, Tad?"

"I found lots of jobs," he came back. "I swept out the barbershop on Bee Street, then the shoe shop on River Street. I culled vegetables for the Piggly Wiggly, and made some deliveries for the Rexall. I worshed some windows at Dolly's Dress Shop, and—"

"Dolly's Dress Shop?" I laughed at that.

"Yeah." Tad grinned sheepishly. "They put me in the window with the dummies, and everybody going down the street laughed at me."

He reached into his pocket, pulled out some change, and placed it on the table.

"Tell me how the juice happened to git cut off," he probed.

So I told him the story of the day he'd come to our house, and we were in Riverbend gittin' permed. I told how we had begged Mama to let us go and see James Dean, and when she said we had too many bills to pay, we were mad at her, and told her to stop harping about them bills all the time.

Tad looked out the window toward the creek, as he snapped a bean into a pan. "So she give in to you? Ain't that just like Aunt Serilda?"

"Nobody forced her," I said snippily.

"Yeah, she coulda been like Mrs. McCoy and gone up the side of y'all's heads."

In my worst nightmares I could not see Mama doing such a thing as that.

"Sometimes I wish she was more . . ." I couldn't think of the word I wanted. "You know, more . . .?"

I tossed the strings in with the beans, and had to dig them out again.

"Spunky?" Tad said.

Was that the word? I shrugged. "I don't know. Something."

"Well, let me tell *you* something." Tad pulled a bucket of beans down between his knees, and settled back in his chair. "You've been up on the mountain at Uncle Luther's house, ain't you?"

"Yeah," I said. "I been there on Decoration Day a few times, why?"

"You know that's the same house where they growed up together—my mama, Eunice, and your mama, Serilda, also Luther, Warner, Nancy, Clayton, Ruth, Daniel, and I forgit the rest."

"Yeah, I know that. Wadn't there 'leben of them in all?"

"That's right. Eleven children and not enough of anything to go around. I've stayed at Uncle Luther's house lots of times—actually, more'n any-place else—and I'll tell you something about that house they growed up in, Carol . . ."

He hesitated, and I figured he was searching his brain for the right words.

"There's a mystical window there . . . a window that remembers . . ."

"A window that remembers?" I repeated careful, just to make sure I heard him right.

"I'll start at the beginning," he went on. "I think I was about six the first time. It was real early one morning. I was at Uncle Luther's house, and while everybody was still asleep I climbed up on the top floor above the bedrooms. It's really no more'n an attic. Long time ago, they usta keep straw ticks up there for the young'uns to sleep on in the wintertime, but by then it was a junk room.

"Anyhow, I was exploring, you know, and I come upon this funny-lookin' window. It's still there. It's perfectly round, and it looks out over the backyard of the old home place, where there's a grassy area for young'uns to play in.

"There's a garden out there, too, that you can see through this window, and some chicken coops out farther away from the house, and nothing but woods beyond that.

"That morning, when I first found the window, it was nasty. It looked like it hadn't been cleaned in twenty years. When I tried to peep through it, I could see shapes of people out there on the grass moving around. They were little like me, you know—young'uns!

"So I thought maybe some of Uncle Luther's kids had got up and gone out to play, even though it seemed awful early for that. I found me an old rag, and I spit on it and worshed a round place in the middle of the window so I could see out of it better.

"Then I could make out them children's faces. And I could see they were dressed in old-timey, raggedy clothes, and they didn't belong to Uncle Luther, or anybody else I knowed.

"They were in a circle and playing an ancient game that musta come acrost the ocean with our ancestors. I could hear them and see them good, even though the window was three stories up and closed tight. It was like a movie playing out there before me.

> *"Ride a cock-horse to Banbury Cross,*
>   *To see a fine lady upon a white horse.*
>   *Rings on her fingers and bells on her toes,*
>   *And she shall have music wherever she goes.*

"That's what they were singing as they played. Then I heard one of them call out, 'Eunice, dance a jig!' and I thought to myself, why, that was my mama's name!

"One of the little blond-headed gals stepped into the circle, placed her hands on her hips, and danced the cutest dance you ever seen. It was from the olden days.

"Next somebody said, 'Serilda, fall down!' and

another of the girls went ker-plop! on her belly in the grass. Serilda was a littler version of Eunice. She was a wee thang."

"Mama!" I was breathless as the full meaning of Tad's story began to dawn on me.

"Then someone yelled, 'Daniel, you're a sheep!' and this redheaded, freckled-faced kid started baaa . . . ing and went down on all fours."

"Uncle Daniel is redheaded!"

"Yeah, he is. Then I heard, 'Warner, shear the sheep!'

"They started laughing so hard. I wisht you coulda seen it."

Tad paused and smiled at me again, then let his eyes wander over the distant hills out the back door.

"All the names of mama's brothers and sisters were called. That's when I knowed for shore I was looking at the past. I watched for a long time that day."

"Did you go back another day?"

"Ever' chance I got over the years, I sneaked up there at dawn or at sunset—that's when you have to be there—and watched and listened, and I learned a lot.

"Sometimes they were playing games and having fun, like that first time. Other times they were working in the garden, feeding the chickens, or just talking about school and church and neighbor young'uns that lived up there on the mountain.

"When I had to go stay with other kin, and I would come back to Uncle Luther's, they would be more growed up when I got back, but the same old patterns stayed the same."

"What patterns?"

"Well, for one, all the girls were older than Aunt Serilda, and all the boys were bigger, so she had to do what everybody said. Aunt Serilda was at the tail end of all the games, 'cause she couldn't run as fast or climb as high or throw as far, and stuff like that.

"Even her mama and daddy, our granny and grandpa, treated her like the runt piglet who had to suck the hind teat. So she was bullied by everybody except my mama, who took up for her, and treated her kind. They were always close, and they loved each other more than the others."

I felt tears come up in my eyes.

"I don't mean to make you sad," Tad went on. "I just want you to see that she learned a certain way to be when she was young, and that's the person she is."

"But she's growed up now, Tad."

"That's right, she is. But inside she don't always feel growed up. I think sometimes she still feels like that little girl who's the last one picked in the games, the one who gits hollered at, the one who has eleven bosses telling her what to do."

Poor Mama. Her feelings then musta been something like mine now.

"But yesterday, I saw some spunk in her, Carol. Did you see it?" Tad was saying.

I nodded, remembering how she had showed her temper and stomped her foot.

Spunk? Yes, it was a good word and a good thing. I hoped Mama would keep the spunk she had found, and what's more, I wondered if I couldn't git me some of it for my own self.

"Tad, we've been so mean to Mama, I'm afraid she's going to leave us like Daddy did."

"Leave *y'all*?" Tad actually laughed. "Only if she ketches amnesia and loses her way home, Carol."

Kentucky came in the back door, walked over to me, and ruffled my kinky head. "Only if the sun freezes over," she said. I realized then she had been listening all this time to our conversation.

Virginia followed her, saying, "Only if that creek out yonder commences to flow up the hill."

Georgia came in from the living room. "Only if the world starts spinning backwards."

"Yeah, then you can worry about it," Tad said, grinning, as my sisters joined us in stringing the green beans.

13

TAD WORKED in Riverbend for the rest of the week, and on Friday evening he took his money to the power company office on Bee Street, and tried to pay our light bill with it.

"We kaint git your power back on till Monday morning," the girl in the office told him. "Our boys done gone home for the weekend."

Tad snatched his money back.

"Then I reckon I won't pay till Monday morning," he said, and left the office.

At the breakfast table on Saturday, which was Mama's day off, Tad laid his money on the table as he was telling us about that conversation at the power company office.

Mama counted the money, then said to us girls,

"Do y'all see what your cousin Tad has done for you?"

Our eyes went everywhere in the room, except to meet Mama's and Tad's.

"Now, Aunt Serilda!" Tad shouted, acting like he'd been insulted. "Is that what you think? It's not so. I would have to say I done it for my own self, and not nobody else!"

"How do you figure that?" Kentucky said.

" 'Cause I got so much fun out of it," he replied. "And I learned some stuff."

"Well, I'm going to insist these girls pay you back, Tad."

Tad shook his head. "I won't take a cent."

"You know . . ." Mama started to say something, then paused.

We left off eating to study her face, where we saw a new light shining.

"You know . . ." she started again, and clutched Tad's arm. "I just had a thought."

We waited. She looked at the money, at Tad, then out the back door at the bright blue sky. "It just might work."

"What?" we all wanted to know.

"Tad, do you think you could do this again?"

"Do what again?"

"Earn money like this, doing odd jobs in Riverbend?"

Tad's face melted into a smile. "I shore could, Aunt Serilda. It was easier'n falling off a log back'ards."

"Let me think, now," she said, with a hint of excitement in her voice. "Let me think."

"I could make even more around holidays," Tad went on. "I might even get something permanent. I could help you out a lot!"

Then it was clear what they were both thinking. Tad would not be a burden if he stayed here. In fact, he was already a big help.

"If you could just pay for your clothes," Mama said. "I don't know how to make things for boys."

"I could do that, and more!" Tad was excited now, and started jabbering a mile a minute. "I could pipe running water in here for you, Aunt Serilda. And I could put in a bathroom. I've seen it done. Then y'all wouldn't have to worsh in a tub in the back room. And when I got done with all that, I could build on another bedroom."

We had learned that when Tad said he could do something, he meant it. So nobody doubted him for a second.

"Now, let's not get too ambitious," Mama said. "A boy needs time for fun, to play his guitar, and go to school. If you could just work enough to take care of your own needs . . . that's all."

"I'm gonna go down to the Pughs' and work off

them shoes he give to me," Tad said. "He's got some clothes there in the back of his store, too. Maybe I can git me some of them for school."

It crossed my mind to say, "What about the Birches?" but I held my tongue. I reckoned it was possible that Tad would be allowed to stay here. Anything is possible. But it was more likely that Mama and Tad were fantasizing, and I wouldn't spoil it.

"I can do lots more than you think I can," Tad said.

"I don't doubt you," Mama said. "But I won't have you working all the time. I would be no better than your Uncle Matthew if I treated you like that."

"I can git a job, too!" Kentucky spoke up suddenly. We looked at her doubtfully. "Well, I can!" she added.

"It wouldn't be right for a girl to go around town doing the things I done," Tad told her.

"Well, I'll bet I can find something that's right for a girl!"

"Next summer you'll be fifteen, Ken," Mama told her. "We can talk about it then."

That morning around ten o'clock, Georgia started reading to me from *Little Women,* as she had been promising to do. Not that I couldn't read it for my own self, but it went faster when she read it out loud. She also took the time to explain words to me that I didn't understand.

Kentucky and Virginia were supposed to be scrubbing the kitchen floor, but I knowed they were not doing any such a'thing. They were fixin' each other's hair, and talking about boys, among other baffling things.

Mama and Tad were busy in the backyard boiling and blueing the white clothes in the worsh tub.

A black DeSoto pulled up to the front of the house. A man got out and come up on the porch. He was wearing some nice gaberdine britches and a short-sleeved shirt that had wilted in the heat. He rapped on the wood frame of the front screen door.

I answered the knock.

"Good morning, little girl," he said politely. "Is your mother at home?"

"Yeah, but you kaint sell her a thang. She's broke as the Ten Commandments."

At that, Georgia pulled me away from the door. "Can I help you?"

"I'd like to speak with your mother, please."

"She's out yonder worshing clothes," Georgia said. "Is it important?"

"Well . . . well, ye . . . ss," the man said hesitantly. "Yes, it is."

"Come in."

Georgia opened the door for him. She always had more manners than the rest of us. She waved him into a seat, then went to the window and bellowed, "Ma . . . ma! Somebody's here!"

Ken and Gin come in from the kitchen, set down on the couch, and eyed the man up and down. I'll have to say he was not hard to look at. He had nice dark hair that was parted neat and clean, and he had large bright eyes that could prob'ly go either way—gray or blue. Some eyes are like that. I couldn't tell how old he was. I never was any 'count at guessing ages of grownups.

Just as the poor man started fidgeting, Mama entered the room. Her face was red with heat, and sweat beads had collected around her hairline. She was wearing her only pair of shorts with an old raggedy shirt over them, and a pair of Kentucky's wore-out sandals. Tad trailed behind her.

The man stood up, acting so nervous you couldn't help from noticing. He tried hard to smile, but his lips stuck together.

"You are Mrs. Collins." It was not a question.

"I am," Mama agreed with him.

"I . . . I am . . . I am . . ." It appeared that the man had done forgot his name.

Mama motioned him to set back down, and she perched on the arm of Virginia's chair. Tad stood behind her. We waited to see if the man would remember who he was.

"Lee Roy G. Puckett," he said at last, as he eased back into his chair.

We waited some more.

"I am a brother to Mrs. Myrtle McCoy."

"Oh, Mrs. McCoy's brother." Mama smiled slightly, and her head bobbed up and down.

"She sent me here," he added. Mr. Puckett was sweating hard as he looked around at all of us young'uns, then back at Mama. "Did she . . . did she . . . ?"

We all leaned forward, waiting, watching. I felt like saying, "Spit it out, Lee Roy!" but I managed to stay quiet.

He did spit it out at last. "She didn't mention me to you?"

Mama shook her head. Mr. Puckett took a deep breath.

"Okay," he muttered. "My sister sent me here because she thought that we . . . you and me . . . we might . . . you know . . ."

Mama seemed to "git it" about that time, but I didn't.

"Oh . . . hh," Mama drawed out the word slow.

"See, my wife, Betty, she died over a year ago. We had four boys. These your girls?"

Mama nodded.

"Such pretty curly hair." Mr. Puckett tried to

smile again. "And this must be the famous Tad-pole?"

Mama nodded.

"Call me Tad," Tad said pleasantly, and stuck out his hand.

Mr. Puckett stood up to take Tad's hand, then sank into his seat again.

Mama lowered her head and patted her hair. "Mr. Puckett, I'm awful sorry you caught me like this, but Mrs. McCoy didn't tell me a thang, and I wadn't expecting—"

"Oh, I know, I know," Mr. Puckett interrupted quickly. "She just wanted us to meet, and since you didn't have a telephone, and I didn't know when I would be down this way . . ."

"Oh, it's—it's all right," Mama came back, and now she seemed about as nervous as Mr. Puckett.

Suddenly Tad stepped forward again, but this time with a stern face and crossed arms. He spoke so loud that everybody in the room was startled.

In somebody else's big bossy voice, which wadn't at all like his own, he ordered, "ALL RIGHT, YOU GALS, GIT OUT HERE IN THE BACKYARD AND HELP ME FINISH THESE CLOTHES, YOU HEAH ME?"

With them words, he grabbed Virginia's arm and started hauling her toward the kitchen, which shore made her mad.

"Have you lost your cotton-pickin' mind?"

Kentucky jumped to her feet. "Right! Come on, let's git to work!" And she grabbed Georgia.

Georgia was too surprised to protest much. "What the . . . ?"

Pulling Georgia, Kentucky followed Tad and Virginia. I set there and watched. I would stay here. That's what I would do. And I would figure out what was going on. Wrong.

"You too, Carolina!" Tad poked his head back into the room. "Git your hind end out here and help!"

"But I have to stay out of the way!"

"Not this time!" Tad took my elbow. I saw Mama and Mr. Puckett exchange a nervous smile as I was forced into the kitchen. Tad pushed me out the back door behind my sisters.

"WHO DO YOU THINK YOU ARE?" Virginia protested in a very loud voice. She was facing Tad with her hands on her hips. I had never seen this peacock with her feathers so well ruffled.

"WHAT THE DEVIL DO YOU THINK YOU ARE DOING?" from Georgia at the same time, just as loud, and she jerked herself out of Kentucky's grasp.

"LET GO OF ME!" from me. I was trying to escape back into the house, but Tad wouldn't turn me a'loose.

Them loud-mouthed Collins gals were just

about as loud as we'd ever been, even without Kentucky's help. Her and Tad were calmly blocking our path, begging us to settle down.

"Will you just listen?" Tad managed to be heard at last.

"WHAT? WHAT?" Georgia screamed, flailing her arms around.

"Mr. Puckett come to see Aunt Serilda," Tad whispered.

"We know that, you moron!" Virginia screamed, too. "We got eyes and ears! Does that make it okay to jerk us around like that?"

"Gin, will you calm down?" Kentucky was saying. "How many times have I heard you say you wisht Mama would git herself a boyfriend?"

"A WHAT?" Virginia was beside herself.

"Are you loco?" Georgia yelled, then again louder, "ARE YOU LOCO?"

"A boyfriend?" I could not be heard above the yelling. "Is that what he is?"

And then there was quiet, a lot of quiet. Me and Virginia and Georgia were gaping at each other, a light finally breaking through our denseness.

Oh . . . hh, so that's what Mr. Lee Roy G. Puckett wanted. So that's why he was so jittery, couldn't remember his name, couldn't tell us why he was there. And that's why Mama was suddenly so nervous her own self. It all fell together.

"Just let 'em alone for a spell, will ya?" Tad said.

We settled down in the backyard, too stunned to protest anymore, or even to speak.

Without another word, Tad went back to doing laundry. Drek'ly Kentucky and Virginia went to help him out, without complaining.

The private conversation inside the house lasted for a long time.

14

THAT EVENING Mr. Lee Roy G. Puckett ate supper with us. Him and Mama both had lost some of their bashfulness, and he told us funny jokes at the table, which kept us in stitches.

We had lots of fresh stuff from our garden, along with fried pork, the usual corn bread, and rice pudding for dessert. Mr. Puckett bragged on Mama's cooking until she blushed and told him to hush up and not carry on so.

I was beginning to suspect that Mama liked Mr. Puckett quite a lot, and I reckoned I liked him, too, even before he announced that he wanted to take every last one of us in his DeSoto, to the show, to see *The Highwayman*.

Of course, Georgia knowed all about *The High-*

wayman, and she informed us on the way to River-bend that it was a movie based on a narrative poem by a man named Alfred Noyes. She told us the plot of the poem, and Kentucky fussed at her for giving away the ending.

In the theater, Tad suggested that me and my sisters sit in the balcony with him so that Mama and Mr. Puckett could be alone. I wondered if Mr. Puckett would hold Mama's hand, but I didn't spend much time worrying about this, because I got so wrapped up in the movie I forgot everything else.

It all took place acrost the ocean a long time ago. People back then couldn't talk English good, and things got so confusing that I, for one, was glad Georgia had explained it to us before we got there.

The Highwayman was the first movie that ever made me cry. My sisters cried, too. Even Tad wiped away a tear at the last where a haunting voice could be heard reciting the end of the poem.

> *And still of a winter's night, they say, when the wind is in*
> *the trees,*
> *When the moon is a ghostly galleon tossed upon cloudy*
> *seas,*
> *When the road is a ribbon of moonlight over the purple*
> *moor,*

> *A highwayman comes riding—*
> *Riding—riding—*

Then the lights came up, and we all sniffed, glanced around at each other, yawned, throwing our arms around in lazy stretches, and pretended we had not been crying.

Driving home, Mama was tucked neatly between Mr. Puckett and Kentucky on the front seat. The rest of us were crammed into the back. I had to perch on Virginia's lap, which put me high enough I could prop my elbows on the top of the front seat and hear better what was being said up there.

We thanked Mr. Puckett for taking us to the movie. We talked about the story for a while, and then Tad asked, "What's your line of work, Mr. Puckett?"

I knowed what he was doing—trying to determine if Mr. Puckett was good enough for Mama.

"I'm a mine electrician over at Grundy."

"Did'ja have to go to school to be that?"

"I took a mail-order course out of Chicago," Mr. Puckett responded.

"That's a good job." Tad whispered this to us, then raised his voice again for Mr. Puckett. "Where's your boys at?"

"They've been with my sister since their mother

died," he responded. "She lives a few miles from me, but I go there most every day, when I get off work, to have supper with them."

"What's their names and ages?" was Tad's next question.

"The oldest one is twelve," Mr. Puckett talked loud over his shoulder. "His name is Isaac. Then there's Samuel, David, and Luke."

"Nice biblical names," Mama commented.

"That's right," Mr. Puckett said. "You see, as a boy, I promised myself that when I had children of my own, I would never give them names that others might poke fun at."

I wondered why Mr. Puckett said that. Could it be when he was a kid that somebody poked fun at *his* name?

"What does the 'G' stand for in Lee Roy G. Puckett?" I asked him.

Mr. Puckett hesitated before answering, "I really don't like to say."

"How come?" Tad was persistent.

"We won't make fun," Kentucky said.

"You see, it come to my daddy like a revelation, right at the moment of my birth. So it was a spur-of-the-moment thing, and I believe he always regretted it."

"So what is it?" Mama wanted to know. Now everybody was curious.

"All right." Mr. Puckett sighed and smiled. "I'll tell you. Promise you won't laugh."

"Yeah, we promise, don't we?" Tad said, and poked me and Virginia on one side and Georgia on the other.

"Uh-huh."

"Yeah."

"Sure, we promise."

"Well, it stands for 'God.' The 'G' stands for 'God.' "

Nobody spoke as we tested the name in our minds: Lee Roy God Puckett.

"What in the tarnation was your daddy thinking?" I wanted to know.

"He meant well," Mr. Puckett explained. "He figured a person with a name like that would never be afraid of anything."

We had promised not to laugh, and we didn't want to, but Tad snickered, and it was contagious. Next thing we knowed, everybody had the silly giggles, even Mr. Lee Roy God Puckett.

When we pulled up in front of the house, Mama said a hasty good night to Mr. Puckett, and we all scrambled out of the car. We understood that she was embarrassed to let him know we had no electric lights.

"Can I come to see you again next Saturday?" he yelled after her.

"Yes!" Mama yelled back.

I woke up very late in the night to the smell of summer rain. I listened to its rat-a-tat-tat on the tin roof of our house, snuggled deep into my pillow, and thought of Daddy. Where was he tonight? Was it raining there? Was he thinking about us at all? Why did he leave us?

15

THE NEXT MORNING it was drizzly, but later in the day, the sun came out long enough for corn gathering. There was so much of it now that even if we ate corn three meals a day, we wouldn't be able to use it all up. Tad and my sisters took a bushel basket into the garden with them for hauling the ears. Tomorrow it would have to be cut off the cob, and canned.

I stayed out of the way and walked to meet Mama. She had her usual poke of Sunday fried chicken, which I took as she got off the bus. I placed my other arm around her waist, as we walked up the road. I liked to be close to her when we were alone like this. She kissed the top of my head.

"Did'ja like *The Highwayman*, Mama?" I asked her.

"It was awful sad," she replied, "but I liked it. Did you?"

"Yeah, I liked the ghost at the end."

"What ghost?"

"Oh, you know the voice tells you about the ghost of the highwayman—that he still comes riding on a winter's night."

Mama said nothing.

"Don't you believe in ghosts, Mama?"

"No, not really."

I was surprised. "You don't think the spirits of the dead are roaming the earth, haunting the living?"

"No, I don't."

"So you don't think there's ghosts in the dark, trying to git you?"

"No, Carol, there are no ghosts."

"How do you know there's not?"

"I just know. Ghost stories are for entertainment, that's all."

"But you've always told us we should keep an open mind, Mama."

"That's right, it's good to keep an open mind, Carolina, but you have to be careful you don't let your brains fall out."

We reached the house just before the storm hit good. Rain come down hard this time, whipping up puddles in the road and slashing summer greenery all over the windows. Darkness creeped in long before it was due.

Kentucky brung out one candle, which she'd been saving. She lit it from the stove and propped it on the kitchen table. It felt good, cozy, right, to be in our little house, out of the weather, with Mama and Tad and my sisters.

As Mama was getting supper on the table, Georgia insisted on reading aloud "The Highwayman," which she had found in Mama's poetry book. She'd memorized most of it already, and in some places the rest of us could recite it right along with her. Natur'ly, being the Collins gals, we recited LOUD, and with each line we got LOUDer.

". . . look for me by moonlight;
Watch for me by moonlight;
I'll come to thee by moonlight,
though hell should bar the way!"

With the noise of the rain and our happy shrieking, we didn't hear the sound of an engine, and somebody coming in the front door. But suddenly we saw a man standing at the kitchen threshold, dripping water on the floor.

"I knocked," he said. "You didn't hear me."

He was tall, with long gray hair hanging out from under his scruffy straw hat, and white pouches under his eyes. He stood there taking in the dim room. All of us had frozen in place.

It was Tad's Uncle Matthew Birch.

"This makes the third time I've had to drive over here to git you, boy," he said to Tad. "Gasoline ain't free, ya know."

The plan to have Tad run for his life was plum forgot, as this man stood before us, dominating the room. He was big and mean.

"Git'cha stuff together, and come on," Mr. Birch said gruffly.

Mama pushed a pot off the hot end of the stove to keep the taters from scorching, then faced Mr. Birch and said, "He wants to stay here."

"Don't matter what he wants," Mr. Birch shot back. "I'm the boy's legal guardian, and he's gotta listen to me. It's the law."

Mama was breathing hard. She pushed damp hair away from her face. Her fingers trembled.

"It might be the law, but it ain't right," she managed to say. "You beat up on him."

" 'Spare the rod, and spoil the child,' " Mr. Birch quoted Scripture. "Come on, Tadpole. It's time to go home."

" 'Do unto others as ye would have them do

unto you,' " Mama quoted Scripture right back at 'im. She was so nervous she had to lean on the table.

"Ha!" Mr. Birch snorted. "I reckon I got you there, Serilda Collins. I'll do for him exactly what was done for me when I was a boy. My daddy beat the tar out of me ever' time I stepped outa line.

"Didn't feel good, but now I know he done me a big favor. Everything I am today, I owe it all to my daddy. You got to learn a boy discipline!"

On the word "discipline" Mr. Birch smacked his right fist into the palm of his left hand, and we all jumped.

You could see Mama was momentarily taken aback, then she sputtered, "He don't need discipline. He needs kindness!"

Mr. Birch ignored her. "Go on, Tadpole, git'cha stuff together." His voice was harsh.

Mama took a bold step toward Mr. Birch, and started to say something else, but suddenly Tad was beside her, placing one hand on her arm. Then he leaned toward her and whispered something in her ear.

Mr. Birch squinted as he tried to see the two of them better.

"Promise?" I heard Mama whisper to Tad.

"Promise." He patted her on the shoulder.

Then Tad walked over to Kentucky and whispered something in her ear, too. Kentucky nodded and tried to smile, but tears were streaming down her cheeks.

Next Tad walked past his uncle into the living room, and everybody followed him. We watched him take up that sorry old pillowcase and push his pitiful supply of clothes into it.

"I'm ready," he said in a tiny voice as he slung the sack over his shoulder.

"No, Tad!" I cried out. I couldn't help it. "Don't go!"

I ran to him and flung my arms around his waist. He put his free arm around me, hugged me tight, and whispered in my ear, "Take care of my guitar."

He let me go and moved out the door quick. Mr. Birch went behind him without another word to anybody. From the front door we could just make out Tad dashing for the pickup in the downpour, opening the door, and tossing his sack into the cab. Then he raised his hand briefly to us, and disappeared inside.

We watched the truck's headlights magnify the raindrops in straight white beams of light, as Mr. Birch turned it around in the road and headed down the holler.

I felt Mama and my sisters move away from the door without a word. They collapsed on the couch and chairs, while I stood there watching the red taillights of the truck disappear around the bend in the road.

I went to Mama, curled up beside her on the couch, and put my head on her shoulder. Nobody had the heart to return to the kitchen and immediately pick up life again where we had left off. We simply stayed there and cried in the dark.

The rain was merciless. It went on and on. The darkness deepened, and still we stayed put, saying little, thinking glum thoughts. The air was heavy with sadness.

After while, I thought of Tad's guitar propped up against the wall in the corner, at the end of the couch. I picked it up and hugged it to me. I placed my left hand on the neck of it, the way I had seen him do a hundred times. With my right hand I strummed the strings soft.

I searched for the chords I needed to harmonize with the melody that was in my head. At first I couldn't find a thing that sounded right, but when I closed my eyes and imagined Tad's fingers on the strings, I could feel the positions forming under my left hand.

After a lot of fumbling, the chords come to me slow, one at a time. My right hand moved awkward up and down the strings, trying to find the best place. By and by, slow and unsure, my fingers found what they wanted.

I sung a little and faltered, picking my way careful, until finally I latched on to a weak rhythm. Over and over I walked through the melody, and picked out chords at the same time.

My sisters were listening to my struggle without speaking, and when I had it down pat, they commenced singing with me. We set there in the dark and sung a sad song together:

> Weep no more, my lady,
> Oh weep no more today.
> We will sing one song
> For the old Kentucky home,
> For the old Kentucky home far away.

When we had sung it three times through, Mama spoke soft, "That was good, Carolina."

"Yeah, it was real good," Virginia agreed.

"You keep on practicing, and you'll learn to play as good as Tad," Georgia said.

"Tad taught his own self to play," Kentucky spoke up. "Just pickin' around like that."

"What did Tad whisper in your ear?" I asked Kentucky.

"He told me where the money is for the light bill, and he said I should take the bus into Riverbend tomorrow morning and pay it," Kentucky said. "What did he say to you?"

"He told me to take care of his guitar."

Then Virginia asked, "What did he say to you, Mama?"

Mama's voice came out of the darkness, and every heart was gladdened to hear her words.

"He said, 'I'll be back.'"

16

WAKING UP to a clear bright morning, I studied Mama's face, which was pale. She hadn't slept good and was not herself. She gave us no instructions as she left for work. Kentucky walked out with her. She would go into town and pay the light bill.

On the back porch three wet bushels of corn waited to be shucked, sliced off the cob, and canned. Without a word, Virginia and Georgia went to work on it, and I dug the last of the Mason jars and lids out from under the house.

By the time Kentucky got home, the corn was ready for canning. She started up the fire under the black pot and hauled up water to sterilize the jars.

When the power company drove up the holler and put our juice back on, we had our jars full of corn all lined up on the shelves in the back room. So we turned on the radio and sung with it as loud as we could.

While the electricity was off, the refrigerator had growed little patches of mold inside of it. As we were singing up a storm, we heated water and scrubbed the refrigerator inside out, till we got it to sparkling. I was so busy helping I forgot to go meet Mama, but when she walked in and saw all the work we'd been doing, she hugged us to her, saying she was proud again.

We were sitting gloomy in the living room that night, halfway listening to *Perry Mason* on the radio, when Mama said, "I wisht Perry Mason was here right now to tell me what to do. I want to get Tad back legal, but I got no idea how to go about it."

"The McCoys might know," Georgia suggested.

"That's right," Kentucky agreed. "Mrs. McCoy usta be a schoolteacher, and Mr. McCoy worked in the sheriff's office a long time ago, so they orta know what to do."

"Tad has so much pride in him," Mama said. "He can't stand people knowing how he's been treated. He don't want their pity. But if I have to ask the McCoys for advice, I'll need to tell them everything."

Before going to bed, I picked at Tad's guitar again until I could play parts of "Blue Moon of Kentucky." I didn't know what to call the chords, so I numbered them and wrote the numbers above the words to the two songs I had learned.

That night Mama tossed and turned again, and I couldn't sleep good either. I'd never had that problem before. I had crazy dreams, too.

For example, I dreamed Tad was pickin' and singin' "I'm Walking the Floor over You." At the same time, I could hear the jars of corn, lined up on the shelves around the room, sealing in the dark. Ever' time one of them popped, I woke up with the strange notion that Tad was walking on the tin roof of our house.

I would go back to sleep, and hear him saying in my dreams, "I'm walking the floor over you, git it? Git it?" Even in dreams he was clever.

Then he would whisper, "I'll be back."

Next morning, before leaving, Mama said, "Ken, gather the tomatoes this morning. They're going bad on the vine."

Kentucky nodded.

"Gin, run up to Pugh's store and fetch some more Mason jars. We're all out. You'll have to charge 'em."

"Will do," from Virginia.

"Georgia, you go help Gin carry the jars, and

then both of y'all help Ken scald the tomatoes for canning."

"Okay," from Georgia.

"And, Carolina, try to—"

"NO!" I felt my lip go out as I stomped my foot. "Don't tell me to stay out of the way!"

All eyes were on me then, and for a minute I wadn't sure if I had been caught whining again, or showing some spunk.

"I can help, too," I added, with more calm than I felt.

"That's right," Mama was quick to respond. "You *are* big enough to help."

I saw her searching her brain for something to tell me to do.

Then, "You can run up the road and ask Mrs. McCoy if it's convenient for me to come up there this evening. Tell her that I need her and Mr. Mc-Coy's advice."

I puffed up, and glanced around at my sisters. *I* had the most important job of all.

Right after breakfast I walked up to the McCoys' with Virginia and Georgia, as they were on their way to the store. Peggy saw me and come running down the gravel drive that led to their house up on the hill.

"Hidy, Carol, wanna play some jumping rope?"

"No, I come on business to see your mama."

"Busy-nuz?" Peggy squinted at me in the sun. "What's that?"

"I have to tell her something important for Mama."

Peggy went running ahead of me then, yelling for her mama. Mrs. McCoy walked out on the porch, wiping her hands on her apron.

"Well, if it's not little Carolina Collins," she said, smiling. "You come to play with Peggy to-day?"

"No, ma'am," I said, as I climbed the stairsteps to the porch. "I come on business."

"Oh, I see," she said, trying not to smile. "On business, is it? Well, would you want a glass of lemonade while we're talking business?"

"Don't mind if I do," I said. It was something I'd heard grownups say when they were offered stuff. I remembered to add, "Thank you."

I could see all the other McCoy children way out yonder working in their garden, which was three or four times bigger than ours. I set down on the porch with Peggy while Mrs. McCoy went in to get the lemonade.

Mama had told me to ask the McCoys just the one question—if it was convenient for her to go up there to their house after work. But once I got to talkin', I couldn't stop. I spilled all the beans to Mrs. McCoy.

I told about Tad's Uncle Matthew striping his

back with a horsewhip, about Tad running away from home and coming to us, about his uncle coming to haul him home, and about Mama wanting to git him back legal and permanent.

As I talked, Mrs. McCoy's face went from pleasant to upset.

"Poor boy," she kept saying over and over. "That poor boy."

Then, "Such a good boy. Such a cheerful boy."

By the time Mama went up to the McCoys' that evening, everybody in the holler had heard Tad's story. In fact, every time it was told, it got revised a bit, so that by day's end Tad was the most pitiful orphan ever was.

Mr. McCoy said he knowed exactly what had to be done. First he would go to Pugh's Mercantile and make a telephone call to Pikeville, the county seat. He would set up a hearing there for Mama with a judge. This judge would then decide if it was worth his time to hear the case.

The next day, which was Wednesday, Mr. McCoy did his part. He drove down to our house that evening to tell Mama that the hearing was set for two o'clock on Monday. Mr. and Mrs. McCoy would drive her there.

Mama and Georgia were up late that night writing letters to the kinfolks again. They told how Tad was treated at the Birches' and about the hearing in

Pikeville on Monday. Mama pleaded with her sisters and brothers to remember poor Eunice and come support her efforts to get Tad away from Matthew Birch.

"I'll mail these letters at the post office first thing in the morning, which is Thursday," I heard Mama say to Georgia as they collapsed into bed. "So they should be delivered by Saturday—Monday at the latest."

Mama would have to miss work on Monday, and the only way she could do that was to swap her day off the following week with another kitchen worker there in the hospital, which she did.

On Thursday and Friday we were too busy to be sad. We put up sauerkraut, canned beets, then pickled and canned cucumbers. For the first time we wondered how in the world our mama had done all of this work, mostly by herself, on her days off, or in the evenings, after she'd worked at the hospital for eight hours.

Neighbors stopped in to ask about Tad. Sometimes they helped us out with what we were doing. They wanted to hear Tad's story firsthand, and Mama said we could tell everything, but not to exaggerate. Mama never did like to hear people exaggerate things.

On one of these visits Mrs. Pugh brung a piece of royal blue material from Pugh's Mercantile. All of us were oohing and ahhing over it when she suddenly turned to Virginia and said, "It's exactly the color of your eyes, dear. Your mother can make you a lovely dress with it."

She laid the material acrost Virginia's shoulders to see the effect, and the rest of us watched in envious silence as Virginia turned pink with pleasure and strutted around the room.

Huh! I fumed to myself. It's exactly the color of *my* eyes, too, and Georgia's and Kentucky's, and for that matter, Mama's. But you don't see people giving dress material to us!

On Saturday Mr. Puckett showed up bright and early, grinning like he couldn't stop. Him and Mama both just seemed to sparkle when they looked at each other.

With hellos out of the way, Mr. Puckett and Mama settled down to coffee at the kitchen table, and she told him the story of Tad. Like everybody else, Mr. Puckett was shocked. He said he wanted to go along with Mama and the McCoys to Pikeville on Monday, and help out if he could.

Later the two of them went for a ride without a bunch of young'uns tagging along. When they got back, she told us they went into Riverbend and had a soda at the Rexall, then strolled around town, looking at the window displays. This was quite a treat for Mama. Just having a day of leisure was something new for her.

Saturday night after supper, we played a lively hand of rummy around the kitchen table, drinking Kool-Aid and eating popcorn. Mr. Puckett was a good card player, and a lot of fun. After he left, around ten o'clock, Mama stood out on the back porch by herself and looked at the stars. When I started to go out there to be with her, Kentucky stopped me.

"I think she wants to be alone," she told me.

I crawled into bed by myself, feeling uneasy. Would things be different now with Mr. Puckett in the picture? Would Mama stay the same? You go along in life believing this is the way things have always been and always will be, but it's not so. Things change.

17

AROUND NOON ON MONDAY Mr.
Puckett arrived to go with Mama to Pikeville. They
drove up to the McCoys', and after while we heard
the car horn blow as the four of them drove back
down the holler past our house. We ran to the
door and waved.

Mr. Puckett was driving his car, with Mama beside him, and the McCoys in the back. Mama
looked like she was born to have a handsome man
driving her around in his big black shiny DeSoto.

I knew that Mama had divorced Daddy when
he'd been gone for a year, but still I wondered
how he would feel if he knew about Mr. Puckett.
Would he be jealous and come home? Would he
try to git Mama back? Would she *have* him back?

For no reason at all, tears welled up in my eyes.

When they got home from Pikeville, we could see, even before Mama walked in the house, that things did not go well for her. Mr. Puckett was behind her. They had taken the McCoys home first. Kentucky and Virginia had fixed supper, and, without speaking, everybody sat down to eat.

We watched Mama and Mr. Puckett fill their plates, then nibble at their food, like they didn't really want it. We let 'em be for a while, but drek'ly we couldn't stand the suspense any longer.

"What happened?" Kentucky blurted out.

"Nothing went our way." Mama's voice was little more than a whisper.

"Did any of your sisters and brothers come?" Georgia asked.

"Not a one," Mama said wearily. "Not a single one."

"Tell us about the hearing," Virginia said.

"I don't have the heart to talk about it right now." Mama sighed and pushed her plate away from her.

With our eyes we appealed to Mr. Puckett.

"Judge Sawyer refuses to hear the case," he said.

"Why?"

"First of all, he's a neighbor of Matthew Birch, who, by the way, was called in for the hearing."

"Who? Matthew Birch?"

"One and the same. Second, the judge is a hard-nosed disciplinarian, just like Birch."

"What does that mean?"

"It means he believes in beating children," Mama said bitterly. "And breaking their spirits."

"Yeah," Mr. Puckett agreed, just as bitterly, it seemed. "He thinks Birch is a fine, upstanding man, who is a good influence on a juvenile delinquent like Tad."

"Juvenile delinquent!" we all sputtered.

"That's what he called Tad just because he ran away from home."

"But who wouldn't run away from *that* home?" I cried.

"He also mentioned the fact that in our house Tad has to sleep on the couch," Mama said sadly. "That we have no running water, no bathroom, and there are five females and no man in the house."

"What's that got to do with anything?" Georgia wailed.

"He thinks women are not fit to raise boys alone," Mama continued. "Mr. Birch stood right there in front of Judge Sawyer and said, 'Serilda Collins, everybody knows you let your girls run over you, and they have a reputation for being loud-mouthed and unruly.' "

There was a sharp intake of breath around the

table from the four of us. We were horrified and ashamed to hear such things said.

"Then Mr. Birch went on and on about Tad's strange ways," Mr. Puckett continued. "He's heard Tad talk about a voice that calls to him in his sleep. He's convinced the boy is surrounded by evil forces and needs the Devil beat out of him."

"That's not the worst of it." Mama picked up the story. "You're not gonna believe this. Mr. Birch insinuated to the judge that when he walked into our house that evening to get Tad, you four girls, along with Tad, were doing an incantation to the Devil by candlelight!"

"WHAT!"

"Yeah!" Mr. Puckett cried out. "Here's what he told the judge . . ."

Mr. Puckett paused to put a mean expression on his face. He pulled his collar up and his hair down over his forehead, and did a mock impression of Mr. Birch.

" 'Now, Judge, I'm not making accusations, mind you, and I'm not sayin' that's what they were really doing, but they were hollering something about hell, and it shore looked to me like they were calling on Satan to come to a meeting in the moonlight!' "

He did a perfect Mr. Birch, and strange noises come bubbling out of me and my sisters. It was nervous laughter, which soon got hysterical. Calling to Satan? It was such an outrageous accusation we couldn't help ourselves. We laughed till we cried.

Mr. Puckett laughed with us, and Mama finally smiled. Gradually we all went quiet, and simply shook our heads in disbelief.

"Did you tell them we were reciting 'The Highwayman'?" Virginia asked.

"I tried to explain," Mama said, "but the judge wouldn't listen. Mr. Puckett tried to help."

"Yeah, I told him about the movie," Mr. Puckett said, "but Judge Sawyer was blind and deaf to everything except Birch's story."

"It was absolutely ridiculous!" my mama said. "Then when I told the judge the reason for the candlelight, he wanted to know how I could take care of another child if I couldn't pay my light bill."

Mr. Puckett put a hand over Mama's. "Serilda, I wish you'd told me about that. I could've helped."

Mama shrugged. "Mr. Puckett, our light bill is not your responsibility." Then she went on with her story. "The McCoys wanted to speak up for Tad, but Judge Sawyer told them that their testimony was not relevant.

"Finally, he asked me if I took my girls to

church, and when I said no, that I didn't have time, he said he wouldn't even consider hearing the case. We couldn't get him to listen to anything else."

And that was that.

In the weeks following, we wrote one letter after another to Tad, but never got an answer. We figured he didn't even see our letters. We could only imagine how awful Tad's life was in that bleak house where Mr. Birch's own little boy, Eugene, had been so unhappy he had escaped into a painted world.

18

THE MUGGY DAYS of August snuck in. We harvested and stored more of the earth's summer bounty, as Mama called it, but we moved slow in the heat.

The McCoys' goats kept our grass trimmed, but if you didn't watch 'em, they'd wander into the shade, so that the grass there stayed neat and short, while the sunny grass growed tall. So I took it on myself to watch the goats. I kept them wet with water from the creek and gave them lots to drink.

The katydids among the dusty weeds had become background music to every move we made, and we didn't notice it anymore, unless it stopped. Sometimes the sound did stop for no reason a'tall that we could see, and we paused in whatever we were doing, thinking something was off-center, until it started up again.

The black snakes known as racers were plentiful. According to old wives' tales, they would chase you down, but nobody ever said what they would do with you if they caught you. They didn't have poison in their teeth, like the copperhead we seen one time. Still, we walked a long way around the black racers as they slid out of their ground nests to cool on the creek banks.

The blue dragonflies we called witch doctors flitted and skimmed the surface of the creek water. The air was crowded with butterflies that year, and somebody said it was a good omen. The petite ones were blue or lemon. The large ones were multi-colored.

The honeybees were having a busy year, too, filling up their nests with golden honey, which would be robbed from them to go on people's eatin' tables. The waspers, mud dobbers, yellow jackets, hornets, and bumblebees were everywhere, and we waged a never-ending war against ants and gnats, flies and mosquitoes.

That's how our world went on turning toward autumn, even without Tad. We missed him, but we had to put our thoughts on the coming school year—wearing shoes again, baloney sandwiches, classmates, recess, new teachers, and oh, yeah—lessons.

I looked over my pitiful supply of clothes, and saw that the hand-me-downs were getting shabbier and shabbier every year. In my whole life I had never had a new dress that was made just for me. My dresses had always belonged to my sisters, who nearly wore them out before they got to me. I had always minded a bit, but now much more. It didn't seem fair.

It was about that time that Georgia read me a poem called "The Ballad of the Harp Weaver." It was about a little boy whose mother was so poor he didn't have any clothes a'tall. I had Georgia read it again and again until I knew part of it.

"Son," said my mother,
When I was knee-high,
"You've need of clothes to cover you,
And not a rag have I.

"There's nothing in the house
To make a boy breeches,
Nor shears to cut a cloth with
Nor thread to take stitches.

"There's nothing in the house
But a loaf-end of rye,
And a harp with a woman's head
Nobody will buy,"
And she began to cry.

The poor mother always took on Mama's face, and I couldn't bear to see her cry. So how could I complain about clothes? Didn't I know that she would buy me lots of new dresses if she could? Why give her something else to worry about? Besides, I didn't want to be a whiner anymore. So I kept my mouth shut and suffered in silence.

Still, I looked longingly at the blue fabric Mrs. Pugh had give to Virginia, wishing it was mine. My one consolation was that Mama had not had time to make Virginia's dress yet, and on the first day of school all four of us had to wear last year's clothes.

Classes began on the day after Labor Day. Kentucky was entering the ninth grade, so she had to ride the bus into Riverbend to the high school. Virginia in the seventh grade, Georgia in the sixth, and me in the fifth still walked up the holler to the Polly's Fork Elementary School, which was right beside of Pugh's Mercantile.

On the third day of school, which was a Thursday, me and Virginia and Georgia were walking home when we saw Matthew Birch's truck parked in front of our house.

"Maybe he brung Tad back to us!" I yelled hopefully, and took off running ahead of my sisters.

But Mr. Birch was sitting in the driver's seat of the truck, with his arm hanging out the door, and Tad was nowhere to be seen.

"Oh," I said, slowing, as I saw him. "Where's Tad?"

"That's what I'd like to know!" he said gruffly.

"We ain't seen him," I said.

"Don't you lie to me, missy!" he hollered, and I saw his fist ball up like he wanted to belt me one with it. "God punishes liars!"

"She's not lying!" Virginia said angrily as she came up beside me and put an arm around me protectively. "Tad's not here."

Matthew Birch sat there glaring at us. Then he looked up the road, and back to the house. It occurred to me that he'd prob'ly already been in there searching.

"Well, let me tell you something," he hissed at us. "When you see him, you can tell him for me that I am going to give him one last chance to come back home and start acting right. And if he don't . . . well, if he don't, then he'll have the sheriff to deal with."

We said nothing, but stood our ground, and gave him eye for eye.

"I'm a man who'd ruther take care of my own problems and leave the law out of it," he went on. "But you can tell your mama I'm giving her fair warning. If I have to send the sheriff after that sorry boy, she'll be in just as much trouble as Tadpole."

"You can send the governor," Virginia yelled

angrily. "Or the President if you want to! If he ain't here, he ain't here!"

Then she pulled me and Georgia along beside her into the house. We were going up the steps when we heard Mr. Birch start up the truck. Rocks and dirt went flying as he screeched his tires turning around in the road. In a jiffy he was gone back down the holler.

We stood there on the porch, watching the cloud of dust behind the truck. Then we looked at each other and grinned. So Tad had run away again. Good for him!

The next evening, me and Virginia and Georgia hurried home from school as quick as we could. We ran into the house out of breath, and were not disappointed.

"Well, here we are!" were the words greeting us, and yes indeedy, there was Tad at the kitchen table, calmly peeling peaches and slicing them into a porcelain pan.

Him and his grin were a sight for sore eyes. We fell all over him, hugging and kissing until we had peach fuzz and juice all over us.

"Lordy mercy, you'd suffocate a feller to death, wouldn't you?" he hollered, but he couldn't quit grinning.

Then we told him all about his uncle coming and threatening to send the sheriff.

A cloud passed over Tad's face. "The sheriff?"

"Yeah," Georgia said, "but Mama said to tell you not to worry about it for a minute. She said her and Mr. Puckett will figger out what to do. She told us you'd show up here today."

"So, tell us, Tad! Tell us!"

"How'd you git here?"

"How'd you git away?"

"I'll tell all," Tad said happily as he pitted a big, juicy peach and sliced it into the pan.

Without hesitation, we pitched in and helped, eating peaches as we worked.

"When I got back to Uncle Matthew's, he told me if I run off again, he'd whoop the living daylights outa me, and he meant it. So I tried to be a model boy for him. When Uncle Matthew said, 'Jump!' I said, 'How far?' I'd say, 'Yes sir' and 'No sir,' 'Yes ma'am' and 'No ma'am.' And I didn't laugh a'tall. He hates laughing!

"If he told me to do one thang, I done that thang, plus three or two more, then run back to him, panting like a dawg, and waited for the next order. Stayed quiet, respectful, and hard-working."

"Bor . . . ing!" Georgia said.

"Uncle Matthew's pet peeve usta be me wasting time on the guitar, but I didn't have it with me, so he couldn't complain about that no more."

"Did he beat you anyhow?" Virginia said, and we all held our breath.

"What do you think?" Tad said.

"What for?" we moaned.

"Well, see, I made me a slingshot, just for fun, you know. A feller's gotta do *something* for fun. And I killed a rooster with it."

"Tad! You killed a rooster?"

"Yeah, shot 'im in the head. Not just any old rooster either. It was Uncle Matthew's pride and joy, best rooster he said he ever had."

"Why'd you kill it?"

"It was an accident! I can't hit the broad side of a barn with a slingshot, much less a moving target. If I'd been aiming at that rooster, he'd still be alive today."

"What were you aiming at?" I asked.

"The broad side of the barn!"

We got the silly giggles.

"I tried to tell Uncle Matthew it was an accident," Tad went on, laughing along with us. "I ast him, 'Now, who would kill a rooster on purpose?' Anyhow, he ordered me to go out and cut him a big old hickory switch."

"He switched you?"

"Oh, Tad . . ."

He took in our stricken faces.

"Aw, shucks! It didn't hurt none!" he assured us, and squared his shoulders, like he was aligning the wounds hidden there under his shirt. "I was almost relieved when it happened.

"See, I had done told myself, I said, 'Self, I'll stay here and be as good as poor li'l ole Eugene usta be, until Uncle Matthew takes up beating on me again, and then I'm hittin' the road for Polly's Fork.'

"But after he switched me, he watched me like a hawk. Wouldn't let me out of his sight. He knowed what I was planning. When school started, I had my chance. He woulda kept me outa school, but the law won't let him.

"So, like a good boy, I caught the school bus, and rode it to the Feds Creek schoolhouse. When I got there, I went in the front door, just in case Uncle Matthew was watching, or had somebody else watching. And I went right on through the building, and out the back door.

"I walked through the woods to the highway, hitched a ride with this old feller from South Carolina, and well, here we are!"

"But that was Tuesday, Tad. This is Friday. You been on the road all this time?" Georgia asked.

"Here's how it was," Tad explained. "This old feller had him one of them big trucks full of peaches, trying to sell 'em. I bet he had a hundred bushels of peaches on that thang. He had drove all the way up here from the sandhills of South Carolina to sell peaches for his brother, who owns a whole orchard down there. This old man looked like he was too old to be driving, much less lifting a bushel basket full of peaches, so I struck him a deal.

"I told him, I said, 'Liberty'—that was his name—I said, 'Liberty, I'll help you out with these here peaches if, when we're done, you'll take me to my Aunt Serilda's house over at Polly's Fork, and give me the last bushel of peaches t'boot.'

"And he was tickled to do it. I been with him since Tuesday."

"How come it took you three days?" Virginia wanted to know.

"It took that long to sell all the peaches," Tad explained. "We had a big sign on each side of the truck that said PEACHES FOR SALE $1.00 BUSHEL, and we'd drive up and down the hollers slow. People would wave at us if they wanted to buy."

"What did'ja eat and where'd you sleep?" Virginia wanted to know.

"For one thang, I ate a lot of peaches, but also Liberty bought me pop and sandwiches at the stores along the way. He was good to me. At night we'd sleep out under the stars, and it wadn't bad a'tall. In fact, it was lots better than sleeping in Uncle Matthew's dark old cave of a house.

"Liberty also had this sweet li'l ole dawg with him. It was a beagle named Ike—after the President. At night, if Ike smelled or heard anything out of the ordinary, he'd bark. I'd like to have me a dawg like that to warn me if Uncle Matthew was coming. You wouldn't hardly believe how much Liberty loved that dawg."

We sat there smiling and shaking our heads. Leave it to Tad, we were thinking, to find adventure wherever he went.

When Kentucky got home, Tad had to go through the same story again, and then one more time for Mama at the supper table.

"We are going to keep an eye out for your uncle," Mama told him.

"Or the sheriff," Tad said glumly.

"I don't believe for a minute he'll send the sheriff," Mama said, "but no matter who comes for you, we are not going to get caught like before. This time, when we see him coming, you are going to run through the woods up to one of the neighbors. Any one of them will hide you. They said so."

Then Mama told him all about going to see the judge, which Tad knew nothing about. He hadn't received our letters either.

"I hate to think of you out there alone on the road, Tad," Mama said. "I'm glad this Liberty person was good to you."

"Yeah, he was. I liked him a whole bunch," Tad said. "He told me right after he picked me up that

I favored his grandson, Willie. That poor boy died a few years ago. He was thirteen—just my age—when he died. I reckon it like to killed old Liberty when he lost Willie.

"He got fond of me real quick. We talked about life and stuff, and I found myself telling him things that I wouldn't tell to just any old body. I think he was crying when he dropped me off here at y'all's house. I 'bout cried my own self."

"He sounds lonesome," Mama said.

"Yeah, I think he is," Tad said, and let his eyes wander over the hills out the back door. "He's got Ike, but somehow that don't seem like enough, does it?"

19

AFTER SUPPER we happily sprawled all over the front porch in the balmy evening air. There was no need to worry about Mr. Birch surprising us, because if there were headlights approaching you could see them sweeping the trees at the bend of the road even before you heard the engine.

Tad strapped on the guitar and wiped his hands on his britches. I noticed that his knees were almost out of them, and he had not one change of clothes with him.

But he wadn't even thinking about britches right then. He was talking about how much he'd missed pickin' and singin', and couldn't wait to get started again. With the usual grin on his impish face, he jumped right in there, and I watched every move he made on the guitar.

> Don't let the stars get in your eyes,
> Don't let the moon break your heart!
> Love blooms at night, in daylight it dies . . .
> When the stars come out,
> Remember you are mine!

After he'd been playing for a while, he paused to take a drink of water, and Kentucky turned to me. "Carol, show Tad what you learned on his guitar."

"Aw, no." I was feeling bashful. "I don't want to."

Before I had the words out of my mouth, Tad was hanging the guitar strap over my thin shoulders.

"Go on now, show me."

So I played "My Old Kentucky Home" and the other tunes I'd picked out by myself. He didn't say a word as he watched me and listened. When I was done, my sisters clapped and Tad gave a shrill whistle through his teeth.

"I'm impressed as all git out!" he hollered. "Who woulda thunk it?"

I didn't know quite how to act, but I did know that praise was a thing I could get used to.

"I'll learn you the names of them chords and show you some more," Tad said. "Then all you'll have to do is practice. You got the hardest part licked a'ready."

After while the neighbors started dropping by. There were McCoys, Pughs, Mills, Hatfields, Cottons, Boultons, and Springs on our premises, once again keeping time to Tad's music, singing along, or dancing in the road.

By this time, everybody had heard about the hearing, and Judge Sawyer had become the booger man. But for an evening nobody talked about him.

Mr. Puckett came on Saturday as usual. Him and Tad greeted each other like old friends, and he told Tad he was going to do whatever he could to help Mama keep him away from his uncle.

So even with one eye on the road that weekend, looking out for Mr. Birch or the sheriff, everybody was in a jolly mood. My feet didn't touch the ground, 'cause Tad spent a lot of time with me, teaching me to play the guitar. He was a good teacher, and I learned fast. In fact, I couldn't get enough of it. I wanted to play day and night. When Tad was picking and singing, I sung along, harmonizing with him.

On Sunday evening, Mama politely suggested we set ourselves down at the kitchen table and do our lessons for the next day. Me and my sisters always took our schoolwork serious, and we commenced studying quiet, as Mama took Tad into the living room to talk to him.

Above the scratching of our pencils on paper, and turning of pages, we could hear her telling him that she was afraid to let him go to school just yet.

"It'll be easy for your uncle to find you there, and it'll be hard for you to get away. You stay close to home this week. Maybe next week you can go and enroll."

"Whatever you say, Aunt Serilda," he agreed cheerfully.

So instead of starting school the next day, Tad went up to Pugh's Mercantile, and bargained with Mr. Pugh for clothes. He brung home two new pairs of pants, two new shirts, a jacket, underwear, and socks. He would work at the store whenever he could, until the clothes were paid off.

It was carnival week, as it was every year at this time, but Mama did not have the money for us to go. We were disappointed, but we didn't beg or whine. We had learned a hard lesson.

Tad didn't say a word about it, but when we got home from school on Tuesday evening, we found he had gone out to the fairgrounds and got a job there in exchange for a whole mess of free passes.

"What about your Uncle Matthew?" Mama asked, with a worried expression. "Don't you think he might go and see you there?"

Tad laughed. "I know you're foolin' me. Uncle Matthew and Aunt Lucy never went to a carnival in their lives. It's another one of them things he calls a waste of time."

The next question was transportation, but Tad told us the Black and White Transit was running a bus hourly to the fairgrounds far into the night.

"I got enough passes for Mr. Puckett and his boys if they wanna go," Tad told Mama. "Want me to go up to Pugh's and call him for you?"

Mama said that was a good idea, so Tad went to call Mr. Puckett.

Later he came home and told Mama, "Mr. Puckett said him and his boys will come early Saturday evening, and they'll bring supper with 'em, so you're not to worry about cooking."

As for his carnival job, Tad wouldn't tell us what it was all about. The only explanation we got was, "You'll find out when you git there."

On Saturday afternoon Mr. Puckett showed up with his four boys. They had stopped on the way to pick up hot dogs, buns, chili, potato chips, and Pepsi-Colas for everybody. What a treat!

Isaac, David, Luke, and Samuel were as cute

and charming as their daddy. With eleven people in our tiny kitchen, supper was a big old noisy jumble. There was a lot of joking and laughing, teasing and getting to know each other. I started thinking it might be fun to have four stepbrothers.

Tad was scheduled for work at 6 p.m., so we had to rush out and leave the kitchen in a mess. Mr. Puckett had borrowed a pickup truck from his cousin, and except for Kentucky and Mama, who climbed up in the cab with Mr. Puckett, the rest of us piled into the back.

We acted real silly, waving and hollering at people along the way, but we were a happy bunch. Once at the fairgrounds, Tad left us, going his merry way, with a promise to meet us later.

I had been to the carnival before, but this time, with so many people, it was more fun than it had ever been. Mr. Puckett paid for everybody to ride the Ferris wheel and the Tilt-A-Whirl. Then him and Mama together bought Sno-Kones for us.

As we went strolling down the fairway, taking in the sights, the smells of cotton candy, popcorn, car'mel apples, and fried onions hung like touchable things in the warm night air. We were nearing the freak shows.

It was hard to pick out one sound above the

noise of children screaming on the rides, and the blare of a different tune from every attraction, not to mention the loud conversations from the sticky, jostling bodies around us. But even with all that, there was one distinct sound that made its way to my ear.

It was a familiar voice squawking, "Step right up, ladies and gentlemen. See the bearded lady up close. Only ten cents will git you in here.

"And while you're at it, take a peek at the littlest man in the world. He'll fit inside of a peck bucket—no foolin'! I seen him with my own two eyeballs!"

So Tad was a carnival barker. There was real excitement in his voice, and he had collected quite a crowd with his lively performance. In fact, he was a show in itself, and it was clear folks were getting a big kick out of him. When he saw us, he flashed his famous grin, and waved. I puffed up, hoping some of my school friends had seen.

"Step right up here, ladies and gentlemen! This is the entryway into the most unusual, the most extra*h* . . . ord . . . inary sights you will ever be lucky enough to see!

"You ain't seen nothing till you've seen the snake lady with scales up and down her back— honest to God! And the ape-man with hair all over his body! I'll tell you what's the truth—this show will give you something to talk about for the rest of your natural-born days!"

He was having the time of his life, and if I hadn't realized it before, it was made clear to me right then and there—Tad was born for show business.

20

BY MONDAY MORNING there hadn't been a sign of Tad's Uncle Matthew or the sheriff, but Mama was still nervous about sending Tad off to school just yet.

"Let's hope your uncle will give up," Mama told him. "If we don't hear anything by next Monday, we'll let you go then."

"Okay," Tad agreed. "Then I'll work for Mr. Pugh a couple hours each day this week."

On Thursday evening, Tad came running in the house from his job, all excited about something. He grabbed his guitar and ran out on the porch with it. I followed.

"Bill Monroe and the Blue Grass Boys are coming to the Morgan Theater!" he explained to me as he settled down to play. "This Saturday! The day after tomorrow!"

"No foolin'? Where'd you hear that?"

"On the radio, and also there's a flyer advertising it up at the store."

He strapped on his guitar.

"How much does it cost to git in?" I asked.

"Nothing if you're in the talent contest."

"What talent contest?"

"After their performance at eleven o'clock on Saturday morning—and it's going to be live on the radio, too—they're having a talent contest. Anybody can enter, and the first prize is five dollars!"

"Wow, five dollars! You're sure to win it, Tad."

"You think so?" He was grinning. He knew so. He always did what he set out to do.

"Natur'ly," I said.

Tad started practicing right then.

After he had sung through one song three or four times, Tad said, "I want to do this song 'cause it's real popular, but it needs something more."

He picked and hummed. "Maybe some fancy finger work." He tried that, then said, "No, that's not right either."

He turned to me. "It's a big hit right now, but it really don't make a good solo, does it?"

"It sounds kinda thin," I agreed.

"Try some harmony on the chorus," he suggested.

So he sung through it again, as I harmonized with him. For variety he went solo on the refrain.

> "Oh, me! Oh gee!
> Perhaps you'd notice me
> If I wadn't drivin' this Model T!"

Then I joined him again.

> "I was looking back to see if you were looking back to see
> If I was looking back to see if you were looking back at
>   me!
> You were cute as you could be, standing looking back at
>   me,
> And it was plain to see that I'd enjoy your com . . . pa
>   . . . ny!"

"That's it!" Tad hollered. "It sounds real good, Carolina. You'll have to sing it with me in the contest."

"In public?" My insides started fluttering.

"Yeah, you and me in front of an audience, and on the radio, too!"

"But I've never done anything like that before!" I halfheartedly objected, while deep inside I realized I *wanted* to do this so bad!

"There's always a first time for everything," he said. "Let's sing it again."

We went through the whole song one more time, and I did my very best. The way Tad grinned at me made me feel like I had sprouted wings.

He was excited. "If we can do that good in the talent contest, we'll be sure to win!"

Dazed, I looked up at the hills that had been in front of me all my life, but suddenly they were taller, greener, more majestic. And there—right there, riding against a perfect September sky, rose one bird, stretching its wings high . . . higher! It was only a small bird, but it could fly places. And it could sing!

When Tad broke the news to Mama at the supper table, she started fretting, which kinda irritated me. "On the radio? Aren't you afraid—"

But Tad interrupted her. "Uncle Matthew and Aunt Lucy don't even own a radio."

"Carol is so young. Do you really think—"

Tad interrupted again. "Didn't I tell y'all that Carolina was going to surprise us one of these days?" He supported me with so much enthusiasm I felt proud. "Well, that day is here."

Mama wadn't finished yet. "What in the world are you going to wear, Carol?"

Wear? Good question. I hadn't thought about that.

The room was quiet as we each ran a mental checklist of possible dresses.

"I can alter that little pink thing of Georgia's for you," Mama suggested.

"Sure," Georgia said. "It's too little for me in the shoulders, but it's still got plenty of wear left in it."

"Yeah, that'll be real nice," I agreed, but I didn't convince anybody, not even myself.

"You know what," Kentucky spoke up suddenly. "I just thought of something."

She had laid down her fork, and sat there, studying me, and thinking.

"Mama, I am trying to remember, has Carolina ever had a new dress?"

Mama's voice was a mere whisper. "No."

All eyes were on me then, and I knew of a sudden why Tad did not want people feeling sorry for him. Pity was a thing that landed on you so heavy it was liable to crush you.

"Who needs a new dress?" I said hotly. "I'd rather have a guitar!"

I wadn't likely to get either one, and I didn't know where the words came from. But there they were. It was just something to say to lighten the moment.

"One like Tad's," I babbled on, hoping nobody was remembering that I had never had a new dress. "Because it's real lightweight, and easy to pluck on, and it has a good sound to it that you don't hear in all guitars."

"My daddy won that guitar," Tad offered, to help me out. "In a poker game, so I heard. It's not the best guitar you can get, but it'll do, I reckon."

Mama gave me a sad smile. "My baby."

"Oh, Mama!" I was plum exasperated with her. "Don't baby me!"

Not much else was said during that supper. My sisters seemed depressed, and I was feeling pretty miserable my own self. Why'd Kentucky have to bring that up for anyway, in front of everybody? It just spoiled everything.

After we had finished cleaning up the kitchen, Kentucky and Virginia took off up to the road to visit somebody; Georgia stuck her nose in a book; Mama started working on Georgia's pink dress for me while she listened to the radio; and me and Tad went back to practicing for our big show on Saturday. We got better and better, and I was happy again.

When Ken and Gin came back, I could barely make out their faces in the gathering dusk, but I could see that they were smiling as they climbed the stairsteps.

"Carolina," Virginia said. "I told Mrs. Pugh what you and Tad are going to do Saturday, and I ast her, I said, 'Mrs. Pugh, do you mind if Mama takes that pretty blue fabric, and makes a dress for

Carol instead of me?' And you know what she said back?"

I couldn't even move enough to shake my head, but my heart acted like I was doing the fifty-yard dash.

"She said she didn't care a'tall!"

"That royal blue!" I sputtered. "But, Gin! It's yours! It's too good for me!"

"Too good for you?" Tad practically exploded. "Carolina Collins, don't you know nothing's too good for you!"

And I was properly put in my place, which for the first time didn't feel like such a bad place to be in.

The next evening, right after supper, Mama started making my new dress. She sent me to bed early so that I would be well rested for the radio show and the talent contest.

I was too wound up to sleep right away. Besides, it seemed strange to be in bed while the whole house buzzed softly around me. I could hear my sisters' voices, Tad's slow strumming on the guitar, the chirping of a cricket, the murmur of the creek, the rustling of the leaves, a hootin' owl, the sewing machine.

Mama's machine was one of them old-timey Singers, where you worked a pedal with your foot to make the needle go up and down. It made a kind of music all its own.

In my head "The Ballad of the Harp Weaver" flowed to the rhythm of the sewing machine. On Christmas Eve, the desperately poor mother, with my mama's face, magically wove clothes for her little boy on the harp nobody would buy.

> Her thin fingers, moving
> In the thin, tall strings,
> Were weav-weav-weaving
> Wonderful things.

I finally drifted away to the sound of the sewing machine whirring in my sleep far into the night. I dreamed that it was Mama singing.

> She sang as she worked,
> And the harp strings spoke;
> Her voice never faltered,
> And the thread never broke.
> And when I awoke . . .

The next morning Mama presented the royal blue dress to me before I went to breakfast. I couldn't speak.

> And piled up beside her
> And toppling to the skies,
> Were the clothes of a king's son,
> Just my size.

It was the most beautiful dress I had ever seen, much less had for my very own. Mama was all smiles. It pleased her to give something this wonderful to me.

"Thank you, Mama," was all I could say. "Thank you."

"Put it on, and let us see you in it!" she said.

So I slipped into the new dress, and Mama buttoned it up the back for me. I tried on my only pair of shoes with it, and they didn't look right, but I figured people would be so envious of this dress they wouldn't even notice my shoes.

There were gasps, oooos, and ahhhs all around the kitchen table when I walked in there in my new dress. Maybe my sisters' eyes were wet, or did I imagine that? Maybe I was as pretty in that color as Virginia would have been, but I was sure I imagined that.

Mr. Puckett and Mama took me and Tad to the Morgan Theater in Riverbend. My sisters agreed to stay at home and listen on the radio, so that Mr. Puckett wouldn't feel like he had to pay for everybody.

Bill Monroe and the Blue Grass Boys opened the show with their famous "Blue Moon of Kentucky," as Tad and I both sat there, enchanted, in the front row with the other contestants.

There was something about being at a live show that made me feel like I had a fever. It stirred my blood, quickened my pulse, and put stars in my eyes. I didn't know the word for it right then, but I learned it later—"stagestruck."

When it was our turn to perform, I felt so charged up I was not even nervous. In fact, I leapt from my seat and up onto the stage, like I really had wings to fly. The words from "The Harp Weaver" kept ringing in my head, so that I felt almost supernatural, like an angel, dressed in a shining blue magical dress. I could do anything in this dress!

Tad was also decked out in one of his new shirts, in the same shade of blue. Bill Monroe introduced us as "Tad and Carolina, the Blue Kids." As we started our song, we both smiled big enough to show all our teeth, the way real professional singers do. We figured later that was one reason why we won easy.

Tad tried to give me half of the prize money, but my giddiness made me generous. I told him to keep it for my part of the light bill he had paid, and he decided to give it all to Mr. Pugh for the clothes.

When we got back home, Tad went on to work at Pugh's store for a while, like he was not affected by so much attention. But I was still dizzy with excitement. I wondered if it could be possible that *I*, Carolina the former nobody, was born for show business, too?

21

LATER, ME AND MY SISTERS, Mama, and Mr. Puckett were in the backyard peeling apples for making apple butter, when the Hatfields dropped by. They had heard me and Tad on the radio, and they couldn't say enough about our act. It was nice having somebody brag on me for a change, and my sisters didn't seem to mind.

The Hatfields also brought a freshly killed chicken, already gutted and plucked for us. They parked on the back steps for a minute to talk to Mr. Puckett while Mama took the chicken into the kitchen to start baking it for our supper.

After a few minutes, all chatter stopped, as everybody's eyes went to the road, where we could see a sheriff's car coming slow. I jumped up, run into the kitchen past Mama, and into the living room.

I did a quick survey of the room to make sure Tad had stashed his pillowcase and guitar out of sight, like Mama had told him. I saw that he had obeyed her, and there was nothing laying around the living room that would betray his presence in the house.

Then I peeped out the front door, and there before me was the high sheriff of Pike County climbing out of his car, walking up our front steps! At the same time, out of the corner of my eye I saw Mr. and Mrs. Hatfield scuttle across the yard and back into their truck.

The sheriff saw me through the screen door.

"Hello, little girl, is a feller by the name of Tadpole hereabouts?"

I shook my head. It was not a lie. Tad was not at home.

The Hatfields' engine sputtered and started. The sheriff turned and watched the truck driving up the holler.

"Who was that?" he wanted to know.

"Mr. and Mrs. Hatfield," I said in a tiny voice.

"Is your mother here?" he asked.

I nodded my head and opened the screen door for the sheriff to come in. He followed me into the kitchen. Mama was bent over the table, mixing a basting batter. When she glanced up and saw the sheriff, she dropped down into a chair, her face as white as the uncooked chicken in front of her.

"How'do, ma'am," the sheriff said real polite. He stood there holding his hat in his hands. "I hope I didn't startle you."

Mama shook her head ever so slightly, and opened her mouth, but nothing came out of it. Mr. Puckett walked in the back door.

Him and the sheriff acted like they were old buddies.

"Howdy, Ralph."

"How's it goin', Lee Roy?"

They shook hands.

"What'chu up to, Sheriff, no good?"

"Oh, I'm looking for a runaway boy. Name's Birch—Tadpole Birch. Y'all seen 'im?"

Mr. Puckett and Mama both stood there shaking their heads slow, and saying nothing.

"Well, his legal guardian, Mr. Matthew Birch over at Feds Creek, said he'd prob'ly be here at his Aunt Serilda Collins's house. Is this the place?"

The sheriff studied Mama's face, but she still did not speak.

Mr. Puckett took charge in a firm and matter-of-fact voice. "Yeah, but we don't know where he's at."

"I see." The sheriff's head bobbed up and down, up and down, as he glanced around the room. He walked to the doorway leading from the kitchen to the back bedroom, peeped around the curtain, then turned back to us.

"You're sure about that?" He was directing this question to Mama.

She nodded again. Mr. Puckett walked over and stood beside of her.

"Well, Mr. Birch said y'all would try to hide the boy," the sheriff said. "And if you're doing that, and if you're lying to me, it's my duty to inform you that you're breaking the law."

At that moment I heard a gasp from outside the door. We all glanced that way and saw Kentucky, Virginia, and Georgia standing just outside the back screen door, listening.

Mama stood up and bravely faced the sheriff. "We don't know where Tadpole's at."

"Well, all right, then." The sheriff seemed not to know what else to say. "Well, all right."

The sheriff glanced around the room again, then turned to go back the way he had come. "If you do see him, tell him he better go home. Will y'all do that for me?"

"Yes," Mama said. "We'll tell him—that is, if we see him."

And the sheriff left. We all stood perfectly still,

hardly daring to breathe, until we heard the car start up.

"Which way is he headed?" Kentucky whispered through the door.

Mr. Puckett walked partway into the living room and peeped out the front door. "He's going on up toward Pugh's, but the Hatfields went up there to warn Tad. He'll be in hiding by now."

Tad did not come home that night, and Clementine McCoy walked down to tell us that Mr. Pugh was hiding him in back of the store.

"Daddy said to tell y'all that the sheriff don't believe you," Clementine told us. "He also said the sheriff'll be coming back up here, or sending his deputies when you least expect it. So he says you should be on the lookout all the time."

We still did not see Tad the next day. When evening came, and I started to walk to meet Mama, Georgia wanted to go with me. I was surprised, as she had never cared about walking.

We met Mama at the bus, and I took her poke of chicken to carry. She greeted us with a hug, then fell into silence. That day she didn't just have T-I-R-E-D wrote all over her, but W-O-R-R-Y was there, too.

"Mama," Georgia said after a while, "I gotta ast you something."

"What's bothering you, Georgia?" Mama touched my sister's arm.

"Well, Mama, you told me one time that the Hatfield and McCoy feud wouldn't a' happened if they'd let the law settle their dispute. You said that's what the law's for. You also said we should always obey the law, but now, Mama, it looks like we're breaking it. Are we?"

"I reckon we are, Georgia, technically anyhow."

"I know what we're doing is right, Mama. How can we be doing the right thing and breaking the law at the same time?"

"I don't know, Georgia. I'm not smart enough to figure that out. What I do know is this: Judge Sawyer is *not* the law. He is not even a good representative of the law, and I know for sure we are doing the right thing."

Mama's eyes went to the tops of the hills ahead of us, and she sighed a long and heavy sigh.

"Back in the olden days when people had slaves," she said, "there were good people who helped the slaves escape. Technically, they were breaking the law by helping the slaves, but they *were* doing the right thing. Do you see?"

Me and Georgia nodded.

"That's how I have to look at this thing with Tad," she went on. "If he was guilty of a crime, and we were hiding him from the law, that would be wrong. But he's not guilty of anything. He's just an orphan. Nobody's ever bothered to take up for him before, and it would be wrong *not* to protect him from Matthew Birch."

That week, for the first time in anybody's memory, the sheriff's car patrolled Polly's Fork regular. Sometimes it rolled up slow to our house, where the driver parked and watched for a spell.

The neighbors were tight-lipped to the law, but reported to us daily, saying Tad had slept here one night, there the next night. We managed to sneak his pillowcase full of clothes to him, but we didn't dare visit him, fearing we might lead the law to his hiding place.

We went on with our lives, going to school and work like everything was normal, but we were depressed. We could only imagine how Tad felt, having to stay in hiding, and not being free to ramble the way he liked to do.

Saturday was the first day of October, and a brisk wind went whipping up and down our holler. The promise of colored leaves and pumpkins was in the air. Once again the moon was full, and late that night I woke up with its light spilling over my face. Out the window I could see it darting in and out of the clouds.

The moon was a ghostly galleon tossed upon cloudy seas.

Then I thought I could hear Tad whispering, *"Watch for me by moonlight."*

I slipped off the end of the bed so as not to disturb Mama. With bare feet I tiptoed past the curtain, and through the kitchen, and opened the back door. Just as I started to push open the screen, a figure came around the corner of the house and started up the steps. Of course it was Tad.

We faced each other on the porch.

"Hidy, Carol," he whispered. "What're you doin' out here? You got shoes on?"

I shook my head. Yeah, it was too cold for sure to go barefooted anymore.

"I heard you coming," I whispered, too.

"Naw, you didn't," he argued. "I didn't make a bit of noise."

"Well, I'm here, ain't I?"

I sat down on the top porch step, and folded my cold feet up under my nightgown. He sat down beside me and dropped something on the porch. It was his pillowcase, packed.

"I come for my guitar," he said. "I'm leaving."

"Leaving?"

"Yeah, I saw the man in the mirror. He told me to move on so that Aunt Serilda and all these other good people don't git in trouble with the law. I have to trust him."

"Where you goin' to?"

"I'll walk to the highway and hitch a ride, but

I'm not going to say where to. That way, when you're questioned, you won't have to lie."

We watched the moon.

"Tell Aunt Serilda not to expect to hear from me for a long time. I got places to go and things to do. But I promise her—and you—as soon as my life is on a clear track, I'll be contacting y'all."

Tears welled up in my eyes.

Tad just laughed. "Don't look so tragic. I'll be all right."

"Tad, how can you go on smiling all the time when such bad things happen to you?"

"That's easy, Carolina. You see, when the truth hurts too much, you gotta invent your own truth. That's how I've always got by."

"You mean like the way you kept Eugene alive in the painting?"

He didn't say anything.

"And the way you kept your mother alive through the mystic window."

I thought I saw a flicker of pain cross over his face, but then he chuckled and winked at me. "Something like that."

I tiptoed back into the house, retrieved the guitar, and brought it to him.

"Did you know James Dean died yesterday?" Tad said as he took his guitar.

"James Dean died?"

"Yeah, in a car wreck. I heard it on the radio. It's sad. He was so young."

I couldn't help remembering that it all started with James Dean on the day we saw *Rebel Without a Cause* in Riverbend. I touched my hair. All the curls were gone, and I hadn't even noticed.

For days after, I could close my eyes and bring up the image of Tad walking down the winding road between the hills in the moonlight. With his sack over one shoulder and his guitar over the other, he hummed soft as he went.

22

A WEEK LATER, on Saturday night, when I was in bed, and supposed to be asleep, I heard Mama and Mr. Puckett talking in the kitchen. He was asking her to marry him. When I raised up to listen better, Georgia, in the other bed, raised up, too.

"We'll get a house halfway between your job and mine," we heard him say. "It'll be big enough for all of our eight kids, and—"

Mama interrupted him. "Lee Roy, why don't your boys live with you now?"

"I have to work. I can't take care of them."

"*I* work six days a week," Mama said, "and I have managed to keep my girls with me all these years."

"But children need a woman," he argued with her.

"No! Your children need *you!*" she shot back. "There is no substitute for a parent. This is something that's bothered me ever since I met you, Lee Roy—that you turned your boys over to your sister to raise, and you visit them when you have time.

"I had one man who didn't want his responsibilities of taking care of his kids. He was gone all the time even before he left us for good. I was always the one who took care of the children from the day they were born. I love my girls, but it would've been nice to have help with them. Now you are asking me to take on your kids, too?"

Mr. Puckett had nothing to say, and I couldn't even imagine the expression on his face. I had never heard Mama talk back to him before, and I felt proud. Even a man with a name like God could not run over my spunky mother!

She went on in a nicer tone. "I cannot bear the look in Carolina's eyes when she says to me, 'Why did my daddy leave?' She is so . . . oo hurt by his abandonment. Your children must feel abandoned, too."

I laid back down quick, and covered my head with the pillow. I did not know that Mama knew how I felt.

I thought Mr. Puckett would quit courting Mama after that, but I was wrong. He was back the next weekend *with* his boys, and for every weekend after that. One night after they left, I asked Mama if she was ever going to marry him.

"It all depends, Carolina," she told me.

"Depends on what?"

"Well, now he has moved his children back into the same house with him. He says he's gonna take care of them, and I want to see if he follows through on that. I'll give him a year, just to see if he really has changed his ways. If, in that time, I can see that he is trying to be a real father to his boys, then yes, I will marry Mr. Puckett."

We went to the post office every day, but there was no word from Tad. It seemed like he'd plum dropped off the planet. The sheriff stopped in again, but we couldn't a' helped him if we'd wanted to. Matthew Birch finally made an appearance his own self, but we had nothing to say to him. He was mad as a hornet 'cause he'd been forced to finish harvesting his crops all by his lonesome. We didn't see him again. Gradually the sheriff's department gave up, too.

There were plenty of hickory nuts that fall. They grew wild all over the hills. Black walnuts were even more plentiful. The four of us gathered them, but I was the only one who would bust 'em with a rock, and pick out the kernels. My sisters did not want to stain their pretty fingers. I liked black walnuts so much I didn't mind the stains.

Cold weather brought its own uglies. We didn't get tormented by insects, but the mice found all the tiny cracks and crannies into our warm place— just wee mice, but lots of 'em.

We each got bad colds. Only I got the flu. Ken and Gin took turns staying home from school with me. They fed me hot soup and aspirin, and made me take cough syrup that tasted like turpentine.

I couldn't go outside for a whole week, and when I was able to join the land of the living again, the trees had gone naked, the hills had turned gray, and the road was knee-deep in mud.

We picked up pinecones in the woods, and carried them home in brown paper pokes. They were good for starting fires. We chucked coal out of the hillside and piled it in the backyard. We kept fires going all the time we were home, in the kitchen and the front room, too.

Two or three of the kinfolks sent us invitations to come to their house for Thanksgiving like they did every year. Mama politely, but coolly, declined them all. She was real disappointed in them.

There come a pitiful snow in December, but it turned to slush and mud. Mama was scheduled to work on Christmas Day, so we celebrated the day before, which was a Saturday, and her day off.

That morning Mr. Puckett and his boys bustled in happily singing "Jingle Bells" as they unloaded our presents from a borrowed truck. Mama's was a wringer washing machine, which like to tickled her to death. She said if we did not think a washing machine was a romantic gift, we should remember that it gave her more time to spend with Mr. Puckett.

We ate too much junk, sang Christmas carols, and played games with Isaac, Samuel, David, and Luke all day and far into the night. They were almost as much fun as Tad, but all of them together couldn't put Tad out of our minds. We wondered where he could be on this Christmas Eve. Was he with people who cared about him? Would he get presents?

Cold rains followed the next week, and we went sliding into 1956 in our muddy saddle oxfords that had been resoled too many times. It was a bleak winter world.

Early in the year, Kentucky turned fifteen and took Tad's job at Pugh's. Virginia turned thirteen, Georgia twelve, and me eleven. Mama did not give us instructions anymore as she was leaving for work. She said we were smart enough to figure out what needed doing.

When we usta be closed up together in cold weather, we quarreled over silly things like bobby pins and shoelaces, or who was going to empty the slop jar, or who was going to take the mice out of the traps. But we had quit that foolishness.

The people in Polly's Fork seemed to have new respect for Mama. They saw her as heroic, and they suddenly seemed more aware of her struggle to raise four children by herself.

Things appeared on our porch from Pugh's Mercantile—more dress material, a bag of sugar or flour, a pair of scissors, ribbons for our hair.

The McCoys brought milk and butter from one of them fourteen cows me and Peggy counted on that long-ago summer day.

The Mills gave us some of their pork when they slaughtered a pig. The Hatfields gave us eggs fairly regular, and a chicken now and then.

If we were not at home, our neighbors would go inside and put things in the refrigerator for us.

So we had plenty to eat that whole winter. Every time we opened a jar of peaches or blackberries or green beans, we thought of Tad. Still no word came from him.

One cold night we all piled into Mama's and my bed, and she read us "The Highwayman." I laid with my head against her shoulder as she read. I closed my eyes. I saw the ribbon of road in the moonlight. I heard the highwayman galloping. I saw the face clearly, and it was Tad's.

And still of a winter's night, they say, when the wind is in the trees,

When the moon is a ghostly galleon tossed upon cloudy
   seas,
When the road is a ribbon of moonlight over the purple
   moor,
A highwayman comes riding—
Riding—riding—

23

THAT SPRING we remembered Tad on his fourteenth birthday. We were planting a new garden, which was to be bigger and better than ever before, mainly because Mama didn't have to do it all by herself.

Easter weekend had always been a holiday for getting together with one or more of the relatives, but not that year. Mama was still upset with them. However, on Decoration Day, when Uncle Jake offered to carry us up on the mountain where him and Mama and the other brothers and sisters growed up, she accepted his offer.

Going to the family cemetery, placing wildflowers on the graves of our dead kin, and having dinner on the ground with our living kin had been an annual event for as long as I could remember. In spite of Mama's anger toward her family, she didn't want to miss it. She swapped her days off with somebody, and Uncle Jake picked us up around ten o'clock that Sunday morning.

The relatives seemed more than friendly. In fact, they were downright gushy. Ever' single one of 'em knowed by this time that poor Tad was struggling all alone in a world of strangers, but nobody came right out and mentioned his name.

It was true my mama had always been the runt piglet, as Tad had said, but that day it was clear to me, the way her sisters and brothers tiptoed around the subject of Tad, that they were afraid of her wrath. I reckon they knew she had every right to be mad at them.

When Mama went to place flowers on the grave of her sister Eunice, Tad's mama, a quietness settled over the group gathered there. Mama knelt on the grass, laid her flowers in front of the tombstone, and closed her eyes. She stayed that way for a long time. You could see her lips moving a little bit.

The rest of the day Mama treated her family nice enough, but you could see the sadness in her eyes. When we left with Uncle Jake to go back home, each and every relative hugged her warmly, and more than one of them said, "I'm sorry, Serilda."

Somebody even said, "I wish I had it to do over again."

But that was easy to say now that it was too late.

24

THE TOMATOES were turning pink on the last day of school when Mr. McCoy stopped his truck to drop a large package on our front porch.

Me and my sisters gathered around the package, but nobody jumped right in there to open it—not in front of Mr. McCoy anyhow. It was addressed to Mama, and the return address said Liberty Rose, 1010 Clark Street, Nashville, Tennessee.

Liberty? Wadn't that the old man from South Carolina—the one selling peaches? But Nashville? We looked at each other with puzzled eyes.

"It come to the post office for you," Mr. McCoy told us. "And I knowed you didn't have a way to haul it home. Y'all know somebody in Nashville?"

We shrugged and didn't answer him. Did we?

Mr. McCoy winked at us, like we were sharing a secret. He was prob'ly thinking this was from Tad, and he was prob'ly right. He left us alone with our package, and we remembered to yell out a thank-you before he drove away.

Natur'ly we couldn't wait for Mama to get home. We tore into the package as soon as Mr. McCoy was out of sight.

It was Tad's guitar. Tad's guitar? I lifted the instrument out of the box it was packed in, and heard something clattering around inside. I reached my hand into the hole under the strings and pulled out an envelope that said *Aunt Serilda and Girls* on the front. I tore that open, and out fell three ten-dollar bills, along with two letters.

One letter was to everybody and the second one was just to me. We crowded around Georgia and looked over her shoulder as she read the first letter out loud.

May, 1956
Nashville, Tenn

Howdy Aunt Serilda, Ken, Gin, Georgia & Carol,
Well, here we are in Nashville! Let me tell yall what happened when I left Polly's Fork. I hitched to Bristol,

Tenn where I called my old friend Liberty down in South Carolina. He drove all the way to Bristol to pick me up and took me to his house. Him and me and Ike were living together and getting along tolerble til one night Liberty heard me pickin the guitar and singing, and he says to me he says boy you belong in Nashville. Your going to be a star. So we packed up some stuff and moved up to here.

It didn't take me a whole day to git a job with a band, not just any old band either, the Pickers 'n Grinners is one of the best bands in Nashville. We pick and grin at one nightspot or another ever night, and on Sat and Sun in the day time we play for parties and celebrations of all kinds and weddings and funerals too. Making awful good money. All the fellers in the band tell me I am going to make it big. Can you beleeve it? Once I get on the Grand Ole Opry, Ill be on my way.

I enrolled in school Aunt Serilda so don't you go worrying about my education. And Im passing everything. We got us three nice rooms to live in over a grocery store. We got a real big bathroom too. Liberty works downstairs at the store sweeping and cleaning up. Don't make much money, but I'm making enough for us both.

Got me two new western outfits with fringe on my shirt and spurs on my boots. And a brand new guitar. A real good one. And on top of that Im saving up a big wad of money to buy me a car. Soon as I turn 18 Uncle Matthew cant touch me and Ill drive up there to see yall.

I want you to spend the dickens out of these extra tens

Im putting in. I owe six dollars to Pugh's Mercantile. Pay that for me and with the rest I want you to go into town and each one buy something you got a hankering for. Now, Aunt Serilda, don't you even think about sending this money back to me. I got more than I can use.

Until we meet again, Ill be thinking about you. You better write to me.

Love, Tad

Then I read my letter out loud.

Hi Carolina,

I am giving you my daddy's guitar. You take care of it and practice ever day. You write me and tell me how much you are learning. I am going to have a band of my own, and soon as you are done with going to school you can come to Nashville and take your place in my band as a picker and backup singer.

You wanted to know how I could keep on smiling when so many bad things happened to me. Now you see why. Bad things can sometimes bring about good fortune. If Uncle Matthew had not beat the tar out of me I would not be in Nashville on my way to being a star.

Carolina, here's something you will understand but I don't know about the other girls. Theres a real old woman lives with the family next door. She cant do anything but set all day long. Somebody has to feed her, and for a while I could not stand to look at her for the pity I felt in my heart was too heavy. But now I don't feel sorry for her cause I know a thing nobody else knows. When she's asleep, the little girl in her comes out to play. I see her in the back yard romping with Ike when the moon is full. I hear her happy little girl's laugh and I think of you.

You got lots of talent gal and don't you let it be wasted. My hand is so tard I cant write no more. Write me back, and Ill stay in touch.

Love, Tad

25

IT WAS ON A SATURDAY in June once
again when we went into Riverbend to "spend the
dickens" out of the money Tad had sent us. Me and
my sisters were still not the best-behaved gals in
Kentucky, but nowadays nobody would accuse us
of being loud-mouthed and unruly.

With her head high, Mama the hero led the way
down River Street. She was going to buy herself
material for a wedding dress. She had not told Mr.
Puckett yet, but she'd done informed us girls that
he had passed her test. She was planning to accept
his proposal, and set the wedding date for her
birthday in October.

Kentucky, who, during her freshman year,
had been voted the most popular girl at Riverbend

High School, followed Mama. She was going to buy supplies for a candy party, and invite all of her friends.

Beside of her strutted Virginia, the prettiest girl in Polly's Fork. She wanted to buy a red sundress.

Behind them came Georgia, the smart one, who, it was already predicted, would be the valedictorian of her class. She was going to buy a book of poetry.

And I, Carolina, the talented one, and a future country music star, walked proud beside of Georgia. I was going to buy a pick and an extra set of strings for my guitar.

Epilogue

From the Old Famous Dead Poet, William Wordsworth

Our birth is but a sleep and a forgetting:
The Soul that rises with us, our life's Star,
            Hath had elsewhere its setting,
                And cometh from afar:
                Not in entire forgetfulness,
                And not in utter nakedness,
But trailing clouds of glory do we come
                From God, who is our home:
Heaven lies about us in our infancy!
Shades of the prison-house begin to close
                Upon the growing Boy,
But he beholds the light, and whence it flows,
                He sees it in his joy;
The Youth, who daily farther from the east
                Must travel, still is Nature's priest,
                And by the vision splendid
                Is on his way attended;
At length the Man perceives it die away,
And fade into the light of common day.

From *"Ode: Intimations of Immortality"*